CW00857456

A Match for Elizabeth

Mira Stables

© Mira Stables 1972

Mira Stables has asserted her rights under the Copyright, Design and Patents Act, 1988, to be identified as the author of this work.

First published in 1972 by Robert Hale & Company.

This edition published in 2018 by Endeavour Media Ltd.

For Dee-Dee and James

Table of Contents

Chapter One

"Very restless, my lord," answered the butler, as he took the Earl's driving coat and indicated to the young footman that he should proceed with the bestowal of the baggage. "Mr Tressidy says he has been on the fidget all day in expectation of your arrival. The physician is with him just now and his orders are that you were to be admitted whenever you so desired, since it was plain that his lordship would have no peace until he had concluded his business with you."

Behind the professional mask the old man's face was drawn in lines of quiet grief, though his voice was calm and controlled. It seemed as though he was prepared to thrust this eagerly awaited guest into his master's room without even allowing him time to remove the dust of travel. The Earl's harsh countenance softened a little, but he only said, "I'd like a word with Mr Tressidy before I go in to his lordship. Ask him to come up to my room if he's about."

"In the library, my lord. I will inform him of your arrival and ask him to wait upon you. Mrs Bateson has put you in the India room, so that you will be close at hand if the master should ask for you."

The Earl nodded and made his unhurried way to the quarters allotted to him. Cheringham was familiar ground. His visits had been irregular but fairly frequent, as befitted the nature of his friendship with its owner. Drying his hands on the fine towel that the good Mrs Bateson had put ready for his use and gazing absently out of the window over the spring glory of the rhododendrons, his mind drifted back across the years to his first meeting with Major Kirkley. His lips twitched involuntarily at the memory of that callow young ensign who had reported to the Major in that rather squalid cottage that had been his billet in Roliça. Nearly twenty years ago. He had been quite disappointed, he recalled, by the gentle courtesy of manner which distinguished his superior officer, having expected something much more brusque and swashbuckling. The disappointment had been short-lived. Vimiero had shown him the sterling qualities of the man, both as leader and comrade-in-arms, and during all the delays and frustrations that followed, as the army saw the hard-bought fruits of victory dissipated by a divided leadership, the fiercely outspoken youngster had found solace in the calm fortitude of the older man. Major Kirkley had accepted the vagaries of the politicians equably, and had gently conveyed to his seething subordinate that it was his business to get upon terms with the men of his troop, rather than to be canvassing the rights and wrongs of a distant court martial. The advice had seemed good to that much younger Richard, though his first clumsy attempts to see to the welfare of his men had been received with good humoured tolerance rather than gratitude. His stolid cohort seemed to be under the impression that it was *their* job to look after *him*, and in their experienced hands his knowledge of the arts of campaigning had developed rapidly, if along somewhat unorthodox lines.

What a good crowd they had been! Instinct and upbringing drew him more naturally to the rustic types with which he was already familiar, yet there were moments when he would be swept by a passion of mingled pity and admiration for some impudent rascal, spewed out of a city slum, foul-mouthed and untaught, yet facing up to life boldly with only the inadequate equipment of his scrawny under-nourished body. To these sons of the gutters every kind of crime was commonplace. Pilfering and poaching, if undetected, were accounted praiseworthy, and drunkenness was their only avenue of escape from intolerable conditions. Yet they could perform prodigies of valour and endurance, they could be generous to a comrade, and their rough jokes and salty comments enlivened many a weary mile. Respect for their good qualities had been born in the young subaltern in those early days. Over the years it had deepened to affectionate understanding. He had gained an insight into the feelings and difficulties of the lower orders that was rare indeed in a man of his class.

For several long moments he stood gazing out of the window, his eyes blind to the lovely flaunt of blossom on which they rested, as his inward vision reviewed the kaleidoscopic medley of figures that revolved about the steadfast presence of Major Kirkley. Though his visits to Cheringham had been less frequent since he had sold out in '16 and had found himself increasingly occupied with the cares of his own wide domains, yet how he was going to miss the serene unchanging friendliness which had always enveloped him as soon as he crossed its hospitable threshold. For the message which had summoned him had been painfully explicit. His friend had but little time left, perhaps only a few days, and would ask a service of him before bidding him farewell. The Earl had not lingered upon his going, as three exhausted teams stabled along the route would testify, and he a man notoriously careful of his cattle.

A quiet knock upon his door broke into the reverie, and he turned to bid Mr Tressidy enter. Greeting exchanged, the secretary was able to supply further details as to the Viscount Cheringham's illness, and to endorse the butler's remarks as to the impatience with which he was awaiting his friend's arrival. The doctor had just left, but had promised to return at nightfall.

"You will come to him soon, won't you, my lord?" the secretary urged. "Indeed I fear he will have no rest until he has unburdened his mind to you. He refuses to take the drops that have been prescribed to ease his pain lest they should cloud his wits and prevent him from explaining his need and his wishes to your lordship."

The Earl surveyed him thoughtfully, tossing the towel into a linen basket and pausing to remove a thread of lint from his coat sleeve. "At once," he said quietly. "But in the interest of sparing Lord Cheringham's strength, can you give me any notion of what service he requires of me?"

Quentin Tressidy's face was a study. The composure which had masked his grief and inward perturbation during the brief interchange broke up. He looked positively ill at ease, almost furtive. "Why, Sir," he stammered, even his meticulous formalities forgotten in his dismay, "I do indeed know something of what his lordship wishes. But it is so unexpected, so recently learned, that I cannot even now believe—in short, my lord," he pulled himself together into some form of coherence, "the matter is of so strange and so intimate a nature that I must beg you to hold me excused. His lordship needed my assistance in securing copies of certain documents. Had this not been the case, I am assured that he would not have divulged a secret that has been buried these twenty years and more."

The Earl found his own curiosity stirred by these half-disclosures. He had not supposed that his old friend's past held a mystery that could have so discomposed his staid and devoted secretary. "Then I will wait upon him without further delay," he said, and led the way from the India room to the vast bedchamber where Viscount Cheringham lay propped against his pillows, his weary gaze flickering hungrily towards the opening door, his pale lips curving to a smile of welcome.

"Why, Sir! It seems I find you in sad case," said the Earl, stooping over the bed and clasping the sick man's hand in his own cool firm one. "Disobeying orders, too," he added, lifting the medicine glass from the table. "I dare swear your doctor bade you swallow this evil-looking potion, did he not? Yes—I thought as much—" noting the wry twist of Lord Cheringham's lips and the infinitesimal shrug of his shoulders. "Let me hold it for you."

His solicitude was gently but quite firmly rejected. "No, Richard. Let be. I must make my dispositions first. Make all safe. Time enough then for potions—and sleep." The voice was a mere thread, but the Earl made no further protest.

"As you wish, Sir," he said quietly. "You know my will to serve you. Only tell me how I may do so."

The dark eyes were lambent with confident affection as they gazed up into the cool grey ones. "Yes, I know," whispered Lord Cheringham. "Quentin, set a chair for Colonel—" He broke off, smiling faintly. "You see, my wits are wandering already. And the papers, Quentin—put them here to my hand. Then you may leave us. No, stay. Have Pennypool bring up the Madeira. My apologies, Richard. I am grown sadly neglectful."

"It is quite shocking," agreed the Earl solemnly. "I cannot think why I put up with you. However, I think, with your permission, we will dispense with the Madeira. It will keep until you have given me your instructions, and then we may enjoy it at our leisure."

There was the ghost of a rueful twinkle in the dark eyes. "As you wish, dear fellow, though I fear you are more like to call for the brandy!"

"Good God!" exclaimed the Earl in mock horror. "I begin to fear the worst. Not—oh no! Charles. Not one of your forlorn hopes? You really cannot expect daredevil gallantry from a man of my years and sober habits!"

But the gleam of humour had faded from Lord Cheringham's expression. His eyelids drooped and he appeared to sink into silent brooding. Then his voice came more heavily. "It's just your years and your respectability that I need, Richard. No daredevil business. Just—a father confessor for myself—and a guardian for my daughter."

Even the Earl's celebrated *savoir-faire* was shaken by this remark, coming from a man whom he had known intimately for years; a man of rigid, almost puritanically high moral standards, and one who certainly had no children as far as the world was aware. He remembered Quentin's stammered phrases. Was he to be asked to take charge of some base-born child, fruit of a youthful indiscretion of which he could scarcely, even now, believe his friend to have been guilty? Through his fast-whirling thoughts he heard his own voice saying, with a fatuous ineptitude that he would have been the first to condemn, "Your daughter, Charles? I did not know you had a daughter."

The sick man sighed. "She does not even know that she *is* my daughter. I have not seen her since she was a mere babe. Even her grandparents believe her to be illegitimate. But she is my true-born daughter, and you will see to it that she is restored to her rightful place in the world, and that she enjoys all the comfort and consequence that my cowardice has so long denied her. It is my earnest hope that you will be able to contrive a suitable match for her, so that her future may be happily settled."

The Earl could not help wondering if this queer tale was some figment of a fevered brain. But the thin hand clasped in his held no trace of heat, and the dark gaze that so eloquently beseeched his assent was sane enough.

"I will do just as you wish," he promised soberly, though he wondered ruefully the while to what sort of an imbroglio he was committing himself.

The grip on his fingers tightened convulsively for a moment, and then was relaxed as the feeble hand fumbled for the documents that the secretary had laid upon the counterpane. "The papers are all here," went on the threadlike voice. "There are copies of the entries in the parish registers. In face of those, no one can question the child's legitimacy."

"Of course they will not," said the Earl, with a calm certainty that was not without its effect. Viscount Cheringham leaned back against his pillows, smiling contentedly, almost sleepily at his friend. "And now that you have ensured that in case of need your daughter will be in safe keeping, do you think that you could bring yourself to follow your physician's advice and submit to acceptance of this noxious-looking medicine? There will be time enough, when you are more rested, to acquaint me with any further details that might prove useful."

Chapter Two

The Earl checked his team at the top of the incline and studied the choice of roads that was offered to him. He had never previously journeyed into Gloucestershire, and had it not been for the tiresome cause of this particular journeying, would have admitted to considerable pleasure in the scene that lay outspread before his gaze. Pasture and meadow in lush profusion spoke to the richness of the soil. Far below him the river looped its leisurely way towards the sea, and all this pastoral display was admirably set off by the dark background of the ancient forest. As matters stood, however, he bestowed scant attention on the beauty of the passing scene but expressed himself eloquently and bitterly on the state of the roads in terms that caused his groom to bite a quivering lip.

"A matter o' seven miles, Sir," said Hanson, in answer to his master's final query. "Or so the ostler at the Golden Guinea assured me, if I understood him aright."

"With these spirited steeds that may well take us the better part of an hour," said the Earl acidly, giving his stolid hirelings the office that further effort was required of them. "Especially as this apology for a road would not appear to have been repaired since King Charles raised the siege of Gloucester. Only an artillery train could create such furrows."

"'Tis at least better than Spain, Sir," said Hanson, "in that it's dry. Do you remember the mud at Rodrigo?"

A reluctant grin dispelled the Earl's expression of deep gloom. "The night we lost the commissariat?" he queried. "Well, I don't think we shall go hungry tonight. From what I can make out the place is small but quite comfortable. It's to be hoped they can put us up, for there are no decent inns in the neighbourhood, and with the onset of old age I find myself much nicer in my requirements than I was in Spain."

Hanson treated this sally with the silent contempt which he felt it deserved; the Earl, too, relapsed into silence, concentrating his attention on his horses and the treacherous descent. He had no idea what sort of a welcome awaited him. His letter had been brief and non-committal, merely introducing himself as an agent acting on behalf of the late Viscount

Cheringham, and announcing his proposed visit. He knew that he might expect to find his newly acquired ward living in modest circumstances with her maternal relatives, who believed the girl to be illegitimate. During long hours spent with the sick man he had finally pieced together the tangled story. Charles had loved his Elizabeth to desperation—but his parents had already selected his future bride. He was only nineteen, and in the immemorial fashion of youth he had been confident that time would reconcile them to the secret marriage that seemed to him the only solution to his problem. But time was not to be allowed him. His girl wife had died in giving birth to their child, and Charles, half crazed with grief, had handed over the baby to grandparents desolated by the loss of their only daughter, despite their belief that she had disgraced their name.

At least no one was likely to contest his protégée's inheritance as a brief consultation with the new Viscount Cheringham had elicited, despite the very questionable legality of that secret ceremony. Charles's bachelor uncle was quite prepared to accept an orphaned great niece of whom he had never heard before along with the more comfortable aspects of his new estate, though he was only too thankful to shuffle off any further responsibility for her welfare on to the shoulders of the younger man. "That's the dandy," he had wheezed affably. "The chit will do far better with your sister than with an old codger like me. Lady Maria will know just how to go about the matter without setting the ton by the ears. Might even fix up a match between the girl and that young nevvy of yours, hey? Been on the town a few years now, ain't he?"

The Earl, receiving the suggestion with the blandest of smiles and an evasive shrug, privately thought it extremely unlikely that any countrified miss would suit young Timothy. At twenty-five he had no longer the taste for rustic innocence. Something much more subtle and sophisticated was required to titillate his jaded palate, and in any case this girl, at twenty-three, was by far too old for him. No doubt when the time came Maria would amuse herself in arranging a suitable match for the girl. It shouldn't be too difficult, in spite of her age, since quite a respectable portion went with her.

He steadied the horses on a sharp zig-zag, and it was at this point that Hanson suddenly said, "Would that be the place, Sir?" and jerked his head to the left, where a single farm gate gave access to a narrow drive.

The Earl contemplated the modest entrance thoughtfully. "It looks more like a farm than the entrance to a gentleman's residence, but we'll try it, John, and see."

They proceeded at a gentle trot along a narrow but well-kept road. If this was indeed a farm it was a prosperous one, decided the Earl, viewing the sleek cattle with appreciative eyes. The buildings were in good repair and the land appeared to be in splendid heart. The man who was running this place certainly knew his work. He recalled that Charles had told him that the household comprised just the three women—his daughter, her grandmother, and some elderly female relative. He wondered how they had managed to discover and retain so superlative a bailiff. The fellow must be worth his weight in gold.

The road swung away from the barns and pigsties and climbed a gentle slope towards the house, snugly set below a beech hanger. Not an imposing residence—just a small stone house which seemed to have grown naturally in its setting, its only ornamentation the line of dripstone above its windows and the modest canopy above its door. Smooth turf swept almost to the walls, where narrow beds of flowers, gay with pinks and sweet-williams, added a note of demure femininity. In increasing confidence that this was indeed the place he was seeking, the Earl trod up the three shallow steps to the front door and set the bell pealing.

His instinct was correct. A rosy-cheeked country girl who looked somewhat out of character in her grey stuff gown and prim cap admitted that Mrs Hamerton did indeed live here, and said she would ask if the gentleman should be admitted. The Earl, entrusting his card to a moist pink palm, thought that the lass would have looked more at home in the hayfield, and since he had not been invited to pass beyond the small square hall, awaited her return with what patience he might and studied his surroundings with mild interest.

They were simple enough. A stone-flagged floor and white-painted walls set off to admiration a heavy oak chest of some antiquity on which was set a bowl of yellow pansies. On the wall above it hung two naval swords and between these a rather improbable looking painting of a sea fight. The Earl was still studying this battle piece through his glass when the serving maid returned to announce that Mrs Hamerton would receive him, and would he please to follow her to the parlour.

This was a pleasant square room with a low-pitched ceiling supported by heavy oak beams and with windows opening on to an orchard. Seated in a wheel chair beside a fire that made the room seem oppressively warm to the Earl was a tiny lady of a Dresden china delicacy, who extended a frail, trembling hand to the visitor and begged his forgiveness for not rising to welcome him. The Earl, bowing over the hand with a vague feeling that it would have been more appropriate to raise it to his lips, after the graceful fashion of an earlier age, realised that his gentle little hostess was lame.

He straightened his tall figure warily in deference to the beams which actually brushed his fair head, and smiled down at her, a smile which so softened the grim set of his lips that she found herself reversing her first impression of a granite façade, and smiled back at him trustfully, taking courage to embark on a soft flood of small talk, enquiring as to his journey and whether he would take some refreshment now or would prefer to wait and join them at dinner, which would be served within the hour.

Before he could reply a slight movement and a sharp cough from the deep window recess, where she had been partly concealed by the curtains, revealed the presence of a second lady. He half turned, expecting to meet his newest responsibility, but the lady who emerged from her retreat was certainly no daughter of Charles Kirkley's. Sixty if she was a day, he decided, gaunt and weatherbeaten, with a complexion that resembled nothing so much as the softly crumpled leather of a well-worn saddle.

Mrs Hamerton was now submerged in a tangle of half-sentences—how could she have been so remiss—dear Clara must forgive her—she had been quite overset by the excitement of receiving a visitor—from which she finally emerged to present the Earl of Anderley to her sister-in-law. Miss Clara and the Earl, waiting with what patience they might until the gentle flow had subsided, considered each other thoughtfully. The Earl had a strong suspicion that he had now met the ruling deity of this feminine establishment and decided that she looked a sensible sort of woman. Miss Clara allowed the Earl to be a well-looking man, and old enough to handle a delicate situation with tact. She wondered what might be his business with their quiet household. Nothing but disaster and sorrow had come of their earlier dealings with Viscount Cheringham. Well—no—perhaps that was not quite true, for the child, Elizabeth, was the secret joy of her heart, though not for worlds would she have admitted it. And of course there was the house. The house and farm were Cheringham's. She hoped that nothing had arisen to interfere with that arrangement. Surely Cheringham's heir would not turn them out?

Mrs Hamerton was earnestly explaining to the Earl that Clara had seen to all their small affairs since dear William had died. She really didn't know how they would have gone on at all without her support, so good and strong-minded as she was. Miss Clara, disclaiming gruffly, assured him that it was all a hum and asked her sister-in-law if she should summon Mattie to show his lordship to his room. The Earl protested politely. He would be very happy to dine with them, but could they not advise him of a decent inn where he could put up for the night?

"You'll need to stop here," said Miss Clara in her abrupt way. "There's no such place this side of Wotton. I had William's room made ready for you, and your man can have the coachman's quarters. They've stood empty these two years since old George died, but they're snug and dry enough."

The Earl believed her. Everything about the place, within and without, spoke of good management. If Miss Hamerton was indeed solely responsible for the running of the estate, she was a very remarkable woman. He said everything that was proper in acceptance of the proffered hospitality, and trusted that the ladies would understand his preference for ridding himself of the dust of the roads before broaching the business that had brought him into Gloucestershire. Both ladies looked a little strained and anxious at this reference, but Mrs Hamerton only said that of course they would await his convenience, while Miss Clara offered to instruct his groom as to the disposal of the horses and to show him the quarters allotted to him. The Earl, mildly amused at her forthright manners, allowed her to have her own way.

Having completed her self-imposed task, Miss Clara did not return to the house but made her way instead to a corner of the barn where she found, as expected, her great-niece Elizabeth engaged in attending to the clamorous requirements of a litter of hound puppies. The pups, newly weaned, had not fully acquired the art of feeding themselves, and in introducing half-a-dozen milky mouths into the food bowls Elizabeth had spattered the thin gruel on the skirts of her brown cambric gown which was also liberally coated with dog hairs. There was a smear of gruel across one cheek and several strands of brown hair had escaped from their loose knot and hung about her absorbed face.

"Good God, girl!" exclaimed her exasperated aunt. "Get up, do! You look the most complete hoyden. Our guest has arrived, and your grandmother has ordered dinner to be served within the hour. There is scarce time to change your dress. Do, pray, leave those wretched pups and make an effort to appear a little more the thing for once."

The girl made no attempt to obey, merely twinkling naughtily up at her aunt and saying, as she picked up a black and tan pup who had been pushed out by his more vigorous brethren, "I must just see that Jester gets his share. Our visitor must have made an uncommon good impression on you that you are suddenly become such a stickler for the proprieties. 'More the thing,' indeed! What will he say if he sees you smoking one of your cigars?"

"As though I would dream of doing so in his presence," protested Miss Clara. "Now do stop funning, Lizbeth, and come into the house. That pup will burst if he eats any more."

The girl got to her feet slowly, reluctantly. "Do I really She had even dared to indulge a dream that Viscount voice. The visit was more important than Elizabeth guessed. Cheringham might have seen fit to endow the child with a

Miss Hamerton closed her ears to the appeal in the wistful comfortable sum that would make it possible for her to marry have to come in to dinner, Aunt?" she asked. "Couldn't I have a headache or a cold, and keep to my room? You know how I dislike meeting strangers." despite the stain on her birth. Surely some honest gentleman might well be glad to marry so sensible and capable a girl if she were adequately dowered? Almost she regretted that she had not tried to induce the girl to follow the standard pattern of sweet insipidity instead of training her as her lieutenant and confidante.

When her first natural grief at the death of her brother had subsided, it had been born in upon Miss Clara that now at last she might enter into her kingdom. The only daughter in a family whose sons by tradition followed the sea, she had been born with a passion for the land. As a child she had tagged along with the bailiff who managed her father's small estate. As she grew older she pored over the books that he despised. Drainage and crop rotation, roots and winter feeding, were her passion. By the time that she was twenty-five she was virtually managing her father's establishment from behind the scenes.

When family duty had summoned her to the help of her brother's wife after the accident which had lamed her, she had found a greater measure of freedom. Completely careless of other people's opinions, William had allowed his sister a liberty of action almost masculine. But he would not countenance innovations. The land was not his own.

And then William had died, and his widow had only too thankfully relinquished the reins of management into Miss Clara's eager and capable hands. With the young Elizabeth, newly emancipated from the shackles of school, as her willing assistant, she had at last been able to put her own ideas into practice. She had succeeded to admiration. The farm had flourished. And if, somewhere along the line, her great-niece had shed the shy decorum of the debutante and had become almost as forthright and capable as her aunt, Miss Clara had counted that, too, a gain.

Now, for the first time, she was wondering if she had done wisely. Elizabeth might fit her present situation to admiration, but even Miss Clara was vaguely aware that the girl lacked the social graces that were accounted desirable in a young lady on the marriage mart. But it was no use regretting past errors. With characteristic good sense Miss Clara decided that a good dinner, punctually served, would do more to dispose the visitor in her great-niece's favour than any regrets on her part.

"Of course you must come down to dinner," she said firmly. "His lordship will certainly wish to see you, since he comes from Viscount Cheringham, who was acquainted with your Mama. So pray make haste, child. We should not be loitering here."

She shooed the girl towards the house, and Elizabeth, surprised by the reference to her mother, so rarely mentioned, submitted with unaccustomed docility, even accepting without demur a suggestion that she should put on her best dress in honour of the visitor.

If this attempt at sartorial splendour was designed to impress the Earl with her gentle femininity, it signally failed of its intent. The white crepe dress had been chosen by her grandmother. It had a modest round neck and tiny puff sleeves, and it only succeeded in emphasising the contrast between the girl's sunburned hands and face and the delicate white skin of her arms and bosom.

Since, further, she was accustomed only to female society, and was distinctly overawed by the Earl's appearance in evening dress, she confined her conversation to the briefest of responses to his various remarks. The Earl found her gauche and heavy in the hand. Her looks he considered moderate, though her eyes, he conceded, were remarkably fine, being of a dark blue with long dusky lashes. Her accent was pure enough, and her manners would not put him to the blush, but she was certainly a dead bore. Plenty of scope here for Maria's ability to apply a little social polish.

Dinner being done, the uneasy little party adjourned to the parlour once more. The two older ladies appeared to feel that they had now done all that hospitality required of them. Mrs Hamerton was fidgeting with a piece of tatting, her hands shaking visibly. Miss Clara fixed an expectant gaze upon the Earl and waited hopefully. The girl had crossed to the window and was gazing out towards the distant hills as though the interview was no concern of hers. Somehow her attitude of complete detachment was provoking. His voice sharpened a little as he plunged into his explanations with less tact than was his wont.

"When you received my message, you would no doubt realise that my visit was concerned with the estate of the late Lord Cheringham?"

Mrs Hamerton and her sister-in-law nodded, a trifle apprehensively. The girl seemed not to be listening. In growing indignation the Earl addressed his next remark to the back of that dark, disinterested head.

"No doubt you will be gratified to learn that he made due provision for his daughter."

Mrs Hamerton pressed a handkerchief to trembling lips. Miss Clara actually smiled, and waited impatiently for further details. The girl continued to gaze out of the window. What was she thinking, he wondered. Believing herself to be illegitimate, did she find it impossible to forgive her father for the wrong she supposed him to have done her? He was suddenly, and quite irrationally, angry on behalf of his friend. How dare this ignorant country chit set herself up in judgement on one of the finest, kindest men he had ever known?

"Miss Elizabeth shows little interest in my news," he said silkily. "Nor, if I may be permitted to say so, does she display even a seemly grief for her father's death. She may, however, be interested to learn that she is not, in fact, Miss Hamerton, but Miss Kirkley. Yes"—for the girl had turned at last—"the Honourable Elizabeth Kirkley." He drawled out the syllables in a voice that turned the courtesy address into an insult—and felt a momentary stab of remorse as he saw the girl's shocked face.

"That's not true," she said fiercely. "I *am* Elizabeth Hamerton. My father was killed at Trafalgar. That's his sword on the wall," she added, as though this somehow gave proof of the truth of her statement. "I know nothing of Lord Cheringham. Why should I grieve for his death?"

"Nevertheless he was indeed your father," said the Earl in a gentler voice. "I have all the necessary evidence. There would seem to have been a conspiracy of silence which has kept you in ignorance of your true parentage. Perhaps your grandmother or aunt would prefer to enlighten you, now that the facts must come out."

There was a little sob from Mrs Hamerton. Slow tears were sliding down her cheeks. Miss Clara, still looking a little dazed by the unexpected revelation, said hesitantly, "They thought it best—my brother and his wife. It was given out that she was Geoffrey's daughter. When they came here to live Geoffrey had just been killed. It was easy to pass her off as his." And then, in an access of bitterness, "They *had* to invent some kind of a story. How could they ever have got the child into a decent school if the truth had been known?"

"If the truth had been known," retorted the Earl, "there would have been no difficulty whatsoever. Cheringham's daughter might command a place in the most select seminary in the land."

But Miss Clara was not so easily silenced. Opposition merely stiffened her attitude. The hint of apology in her voice disappeared, and she snapped back, "And who was to say she *was* his daughter when the man himself had cast her off?"

"He had made very adequate provision for her," said the Earl quietly. Not even his fierce partisanship could honestly defend his friend's vacillation over the acknowledgement of the girl.

Miss Clara, too, fell silent, remembering that 'adequate provision' meant the home that she so loved. What would become of them all, now that the distant source of all their comfort was dead?

Into the little silence fell Mrs Hamerton's voice, tear thickened still. "Do you mean that my Elizabeth was actually married to Viscount Cheringham, and that the child is legitimate?"

The Earl bowed his assent. "That is the truth of the matter, Madam."

"Oh! How cruel! To let us believe, all these years—" Her voice broke completely, and she turned her face away from the Earl, fumbling for her handkerchief once more. There was a swift whirl of skirts as Elizabeth swept past the Earl and knelt beside her grandmother, warm young arms round the frail shoulders.

"Don't cry, Gran. It makes no difference to me. I've been completely happy here with you, and who is going to care a pin whether I'm Elizabeth Hamerton or Elizabeth Kirkley? If it comes to that"—fiercely—"I'd much rather be Elizabeth Hamerton. The Hamertons have nothing to be ashamed of."

The Earl did not miss the flash of scorn in the deep blue eyes, but having once controlled his mounting irritation, refused to be provoked into further unbecoming retort.

"My concern is not with the past, but with the future," he said temperately. "Nor would it be proper for me to express any opinion on matters quite outside my personal knowledge. My task is simply to inform you of the arrangements that have been made for Miss Kirkley's future."

He paused for a moment, but Elizabeth appeared to be fully absorbed in petting and soothing her grandmother. Only Miss Clara was attending to him. He went on, quite unperturbed, "It was your father's wish that you should take your proper place in society. To that end he has placed you in my charge until you reach the age of twenty-five, or until you marry, with my approval, before attaining that age. Since mine is a bachelor establishment, I propose to place you with my sister, who will, in due course, attend to all the details of your début. I shall be grateful if you will make your preparations for travelling as quickly as possible, so that I may see you safely established in London before returning to Westmorland."

There was a brief but pregnant pause. Then Elizabeth rose to her feet in one smooth, supple movement and turned at last to face the Earl.

"I thank you for your condescension, my lord," she said icily. "It is quite unnecessary for you to concern yourself further with my affairs. I shall not be accompanying you to London, or, indeed, anywhere else. This house has been my home for as long as I can remember, and I intend to remain here. I have no desire whatsoever to take any place in society, and see no necessity to bow to the wishes of a father I never knew. If, as I apprehend, you are in some sort my guardian until my twenty-fifth birthday, you may content yourself that I shall be well cared for by those who love me, and who have charged themselves with my welfare since I was born. And since I have no intention of marrying, you need have no anxiety on that head either." She dropped him a tiny stiff curtsy, as though to signify that the matter was now closed, and turned back to her grandmother.

The Earl considered her thoughtfully. On the whole he sympathised with her attitude, though of course she could not be permitted to have her own way since he had given his promise to her father. He even felt a faint tinge of admiration. Roused to anger, she had forgotten her shyness and had rounded on him like the thoroughbred she was. His reply was mild, even conciliatory.

"I regret that it will not be possible for you to remain here, Miss Kirkley. No—do not argue. I quite understand that the realisation of your true circumstances has been a great shock to you, but I feel sure that a period of quiet reflection, together with the wise counsel of your grandmother and aunt, will bring home to you the advantages of—"

He was not permitted to finish. The girl flashed out at him in a passion of resentment, interrupting his measured phrases with scant courtesy. "If you *will* have it without roundaboutation, my lord, I utterly refuse to recognise the authority that you claim. *You* will not permit me to remain in my own home, indeed! How dare you presume to direct my life?" And then, simmering down a little under the Earl's calm gaze, she went on more moderately, "I regret that I should have forgotten the consideration due to a guest, but the provocation was past all bearing. You have only yourself to blame if I have overstepped the bounds of decorum."

"You have certainly convinced me that you stand in great need of proper guidance," acknowledged the Earl coolly. "And since you wish to dispense with roundaboutation, permit me further to inform you that by the terms of your father's will, this house is now at my disposal. It is not within your power to remain here without my consent, Miss Kirkley."

There was a little gasp of utter dismay from Miss Clara. The Earl went on pleasantly, "However, so long as you remain biddable I shall be only too happy to leave Mrs and Miss Hamerton in undisturbed occupation. I am already convinced that the place could not be in better hands. When you have thought things over, I trust that it will not be necessary for me to make any changes."

Chapter Three

"Really, Richard, it is quite impossible, I promise you." Lady Maria picked up her novel, indicating, she hoped, that this tiresome discussion was now closed. The Earl leaned over and removed it from between her slender white fingers. She sighed, and prepared to defend her position.

"In view of her recent bereavement I cannot take her into society, even if I were willing, which I most certainly am not. She is too old to be kept in the schoolroom, and as for your notion that she might fill the place of a daughter in my establishment, it is really too absurd. I had never the least wish for a daughter, and had I ever been so misguided as to think of adopting one, I should not choose a girl who, if I am not mistaken, which is extremely unlikely, is both secretive and obstinate. Indeed I feel positively ill at ease in her society. All she ever says is 'Yes, ma'am,' and 'No, ma'am,' and 'Indeed, ma'am,' and all the time her eyes flash blue fire."

Her ladyship shivered artistically, but seeing that her brother was about to speak, hastily abandoned histrionics and hurried on with her diatribe. "She has no social graces whatsoever. She can neither dance nor sing nor play cards, nor even converse, so far as I am aware. And surely even you must have realised that she is quite impossibly dowdy."

"That at least is scarcely her fault, and can easily be remedied," put in the Earl as his sister paused for breath. She paid no heed.

"To bring me such a creature at the very height of the season, when every day is positively crammed with engagements, and to expect me to devote my time to showing her how she should go on! No, Richard. It is too much. Take her up to Anderley to Hester, and keep her well hidden away until she has learned her A.B.C. Get a dancing master for her, and a governess—no—she is too old for that—well then—a companion, some woman of good sense and good taste who will teach her how to dress and do something about her complexion. Then bring her back to me next year and I will engage to do my best to get her off your hands. There! That is a handsome offer, and it is all you will get from me."

"Has it ever occurred to you, Maria, that you are totally and irredeemably selfish?" enquired the Earl.

"But of course, my dear. How else could one live in any degree of comfort? How else could I understand you so well?" returned his sister sweetly. "For if there was ever a man entirely compounded of selfishness, he is standing beside me at this moment and preventing me from taking a sorely needed rest. You do not care for the social round, so you simply withdraw from society until you are almost a recluse. You dislike politics so you only fulfil your hereditary duties when one of your philanthropic friends is trying to force some reform or other upon us all. You despise women for their incurably shallow and frivolous dispositions, so you have abjured marriage, and it is extremely bad for Timothy, let me tell you, to be given the notion that he will inherit Anderley, for it is quite likely that in your dotage you will suddenly decide to marry just to disoblige him. If that is not selfishness, I do not know it when I see it."

"I am sure you are quite right, my dear," said the Earl with disarming meekness.

"And if you are trying to imply that I have no pity for a lonely orphan, let me point out to you first that she is *your* responsibility, which you have just failed to shift on to my shoulders, and secondly that she will be far happier at Anderley. Her interests are purely rustic. At Anderley she may ride all day if she wishes, and I am sure that Hester will be delighted to secure the services of such an accomplished veterinarian for those horrid little dogs of hers, and you will have the satisfaction of knowing that at least one of your sisters is pleased with your newest protégée."

The Earl, who had listened attentively, if with twitching lips, to his sister's masterly dissertation on selfishness, now ventured to interpolate a soothing comment.

"Timothy, at any rate, seems to have taken to her," he suggested.

"Timothy!" snorted that gentleman's mother. "He admires her horsemanship and talks to her as if she were one of his more disreputable cronies. She permits him to use the most unsuitable language in her presence with never a hint of censure. No wonder he says she is quite a good sort of girl. It is perfectly clear to me that he simply does not see her as a girl at all."

"For that we should perhaps be grateful," said the Earl rather dryly. "I would not care to see him making her the object of his attentions at this stage. Later, perhaps, when she is a little more awake to the time of day, we might see how they suit."

Her ladyship bridled angrily, and promised her brother that such a match as he envisaged would never have *her* blessing.

"No?" queried the Earl. "I see no particular objection. She is quite a considerable heiress, and her breeding is perfectly respectable. It would not be a bad match. And Timothy, you know, is a very expensive young man. But we shall see. Let him come to me as usual in August. Miss Kirkley can practise her social graces on him. And one thing at least you shall do for me. See that the girl buys suitable clothes. I cannot have all the world declaring that my ward—God help me—is a dowd. Now come, Maria, you know very well that you will enjoy spending my money. And though it grieves me to be obliged to pay you compliments, I will freely admit that your instinct for fashion is rarely at fault."

A reluctant smile curved her ladyship's mouth. "We-ell," she hesitated, "but what about her mourning?"

The Earl frowned over that, but finally decided that if the girl was to be kept secluded at Anderley for several months they might, for once, run counter to established precedent. "Besides," he concluded, "I really cannot face the prospect of seeing her about the place clad always in funereal black, and Charles would have been the last man to wish it. Nor would it serve at all in educating her taste for fashion."

Lady Maria thereupon engaged herself to furnish the orphan with a wardrobe that should be the envy of all feminine beholders, and the Earl went off to find his charge and to break to her the news of the change in her immediate prospects.

It was received with complete indifference. She betrayed no interest in Anderley, its whereabouts and inhabitants, the sister who kept house for him or the kind of life that she would lead there. The Earl could not refrain from silent tribute to such admirable tactics. During his military career he had frequently studied the behaviour of the peoples of occupied countries. Miss Kirkley's demeanour reminded him forcibly of certain aristocratic ladies of those countries. The conqueror's presence must be endured, but he could be snubbed and ignored, his friendly overtures not so much rejected as simply unnoticed, until he was thoroughly ill at ease and almost apologetic. Such tactics would not work with him of course. He was merely appreciating the instinctive behaviour that was the outcome of the girl's breeding. '*Bon sang ne peut mentir*,' as the French had it. The Earl was beginning to consider Miss Kirkley as a person in her own right rather than as an inherited obligation. She was certainly not the spiritless creature he had first thought her. There had been, at times, a gleam in the blue eyes that betrayed the rebellion raging behind the icy restraint. It seemed likely that her sojourn at Anderley might be enlivened by an occasional brisk engagement. He viewed that prospect with amused satisfaction.

Since there was no hope of ridding herself of her unwanted guest by any other means, Lady Maria made all haste to accomplish her share of the bargain. Elizabeth was hurried from one select establishment to another. Rich silks and velvets, fine linens and dainty muslins and gauzes were purchased with what seemed to her reckless extravagance. Shoes for all occasions, gloves, silk stockings, fans and ribbons, the requirements of a lady of fashion seemed endless. She soon found it necessary to abandon the pose of cool boredom with which she had embarked on the shopping expeditions. One could not help being interested in the accumulation of so many treasures, and if all had been left to Lady Maria's choosing she would have bought only such shades as were '*dernier cri*'—principally bronze-greens and saffron-yellows—which had the effect of turning fading sunburn to a dirty sallowness. Every feminine instinct rebelled, as also the practical good sense inculcated by Miss Clara. If so much money were to be spent on fashionable clothes, then she would choose colours that she would enjoy wearing, even if details of style and cut must be left to the more experienced lady. Calmly but definitely she rejected the brown velvet that Lady Maria had selected for her riding habit, and indicated a sapphire blue which accentuated the blue of her eyes. Lady Maria admitted defeat. It was the first of many tussles between the two ladies. Lady Maria emerged from the campaign with a strong notion that her brother was not fully aware of the magnitude of his undertaking. A young woman of twenty-three with a definite will of her own could not be cowed into submission so easily as a chit of seventeen or so. But this opinion she kept to herself, fearful lest the Earl should change his mind about removing the trying creature to Anderley.

To Elizabeth the days seemed endless. There were weary hours of standing patiently to be fitted while Lady Maria's dresser instructed the two sewing women who had been engaged to complete her new wardrobe as soon as possible. No entertainment was devised for her, for Lady Maria's many engagements left her little enough time to be grudgingly bestowed upon the shopping expeditions. Sometimes she took refuge in the library, browsing among the musty books that no one else seemed to care for. At least it was peaceful there, and she discovered an old road-book of Gloucestershire with which she assuaged her homesickness.

Only in the early morning hours was there any pleasure to be found in this new existence. Then she would go riding in the park, attended sometimes by a groom, but more usually by Timothy Elsford. They were Timothy's horses that she rode, and with Timothy alone did she a little discard her reserve. From their first accidental encounter in the stable yard they had been on the easiest of terms. A carelessly kind offer of a mount suitable for a lady had been eagerly accepted, the innocent Elizabeth never giving a thought as to why so dashing a blade as Mr Elsford kept such an animal in his stables. Chance had brought him to the park where Miss Kirkley was quite unwittingly demonstrating that, whatever the shortcomings he had heard his Mama bemoaning, her horsemanship was of the first order. Nothing could have established her more firmly in his regard, and an admiring comment from one of his particular friends serving to endorse his own opinion, he was very happy to ride with her whenever no more attractive occupation offered. A light-hearted young man of considerable charm, he kept her in a ripple of amusement by an artless flow of comment on the various notabilities who chanced to cross their path. Elizabeth found herself lifted quite out of her despondency, and since he was so obliging as to answer all her questions with exemplary patience—the role of wiseacre being new to him and therefore tolerably amusing—she was much inclined to think him as goodhearted as he was entertaining, and to count him her sole friend in her lonely exile.

Indeed there was only one subject on which they found themselves at odds. Mr Elsford held to it firmly that his uncle was a very good sort of man. He might be a trifle strait-laced and inclined to view life much more soberly than did his ebullient nephew, and he certainly had an odd kick to his gallop when it came to matters of reform and philanthropy, but there was no one better to help one out of a fix. To Elizabeth's fierce denunciation and accusations of blackmail and bullying he turned an amused but disbelieving ear. She must have misunderstood. His uncle was the kindest of men. When she learned to know him better she would find him the most indulgent guardian, with only her own good at heart.

"I am his heir, you know," confided Timothy, "and though there is not the least need for it, for my father was pretty well to pass, he makes me a spanking allowance, as well as giving me the run of Anderley whenever I choose to go. No, depend upon it, Miss Elizabeth, you are quite mistaken in him."

And Elizabeth, feeling that his attitude, if ill-informed, at least did credit to his own warm heart, made no further attempt to shake his allegiance.

Chapter Four

"No," said Elizabeth defiantly. "I will not."

One eyebrow lifted gently, and the corners of the firm mouth were tucked in as though to restrain a smile. Otherwise the Earl surveyed the rebel with his customary imperturbability.

She knew very well that it was foolish to fall into disputation with him, yet she could never resist the temptation. Each time that she had tried to assert her own will his reasonable arguments had defeated her at all points and forced her into reluctant submission. It would have been far more dignified to have maintained her original pose of passive silence, but she was too young and too passionate to pursue such tactics for long. Moreover she was beginning to find a strange exhilaration in the contest between them. So far, she conceded fairly, she had been outmanoeuvred and discomfited in each engagement, but one day she would emerge the victor, and it was the last battle that counted.

"It is quite unreasonable," she went on now. "I am no longer a child to submit without question to the dictates of my elders."

The Earl, accepting unmoved the reference to his advanced age, said kindly, "I doubt if you ever did *that*, Miss Kirkley, even as a child. Certainly not after you had learned to talk. And I strongly suspect that even in infancy you kicked and screamed whenever your will was crossed. I can only be thankful that you were not in my charge at that period in your career. I should have been quite at a loss as to how to deal with your tantrums at that tender age."

"But not now?" she enquired with dangerous meekness.

"Why, no. I do not anticipate any unusual difficulty," he smiled back.

"By blackmail, I suppose, as usual," she said bitterly. "If I do not obey you, you will threaten to evict my family from their home—which by every natural right is far more theirs than yours, for they have worked for it and cherished it, while you have merely inherited it, quite undeservedly, to add to an estate already by far too vast for one man to own."

The Earl might have pointed out that he had not in fact inherited it, but merely held it in trust for her. He did not do so. It would be a pity to end so promising a skirmish too soon. He relished the battles of words and wits quite as much as did his ward.

"Would you say, 'quite undeservedly'?" he enquired earnestly. "You do not feel that my patient endeavours on your behalf merit some small recompense?"

Her indignant face was answer enough. "No?" he smiled. "And as for your remarks about my estate, can it be, my dear Miss Kirkley, that you harbour revolutionary principles in your bosom? Keep them to yourself, I do beg of you. They will certainly not serve to advance you in your social career."

"As I have repeatedly assured you, my lord, I do not wish for a social career. And I care not at all for all these useless accomplishments that you are so determined to thrust upon me. What, for instance, is the use of learning Italian?"

"It is generally accepted," said the Earl solemnly, "that a knowledge of foreign languages is the key to a vast treasure house of literature." He raised that mocking eyebrow at her.

"Bah!" said the lady. "Don't waste that fustian on me. You don't believe a word of it."

"Really, Miss Kirkley," said the Earl in pained reproach, "I can only suppose that you have picked up this indelicate manner of speech from my nephew Timothy. Pray refrain. It will not—"

"Serve to advance my social career," snapped Elizabeth. "I am aware."

"And do not interrupt me," he went on coolly. "That is ill-mannered. I was about to observe that it will not be necessary for you to acquire a thorough knowledge of Italian. All that is needed is familiarity with a few words and phrases appropriate to the discussion of the fine arts. These, pronounced with confidence and an impeccable accent, will convey the impression that you are perfectly at home in the language."

"And that is what I detest above all. I could respect a sound knowledge of the Italian tongue, even if I, personally, can see little use for it. But to be acquiring a few words like an educated parrot, merely to create a false impression of a culture one does not possess, is what I have no patience with. Pretentious folly!"

The Earl studied her curiously. She was, he decided, quite surprisingly lovely when she was moved to indignation. Maria had spoken of eyes that flashed blue fire. He acknowledged the accuracy of the description. For himself it was the enchanting profile that he found attractive—the straight little nose, the short full upper lip that seemed to invite kisses, and the dimpled determined chin. She was putting out promising petals of undeniable charm, this unwanted ward of his.

"If you could choose your own curriculum of studies, what would you choose?" he asked suddenly, on a note of genuine friendly interest.

She was startled. The blaze in the blue eyes died, and she hesitated a little, shyly, as though she feared his laughter.

"I would like to study the lives and writings of people whom I admire," she said at last.

"And they are?"

This time the pause was even longer, and the answer when it came surprised him considerably.

"Cobbett and Jeremy Bentham and Elizabeth Fry. Perhaps Mr Owen of New Lanark, though I have not quite made up my mind about him. It seems to me that his scheme, while doubtless well-meant, is yet designed to further the interests of the employer. And the hours that the children must work are still shockingly long."

"Dear me," said the Earl, divided between amazement and amusement. "For a female you seem to be remarkably well informed. May I ask who has helped to guide your tastes in social philosophy?"

"My Aunt Clara, my lord, was an admirer of Mr Cobbett, having once heard him declare that the best religion was one that gave all men plenty to eat and drink. Of late there has been much hardship in rural parts, and to my aunt, who would never refuse food to even the most idle and impudent of beggars, this pronouncement seemed to embody a sound and whole philosophy. I have, perhaps, travelled a little further than my aunt upon the path towards liberal reform," finished the lady sedately.

Amusement won. He could not forbear a little gentle teasing. "I had thought to hear a young lady set up Wellington or, perhaps, since you were bred in the naval tradition, Lord Nelson as your heroes," he suggested. "Unless, of course, you preferred the high romantical, and worshipped at the shrine of the late Lord Byron."

"I have little taste for poetry," said Elizabeth demurely. "And while I must admire the valour of both the Duke and Lord Nelson and truly value their devoted services to their country, yet I cannot like the Duke's politics, nor approve Lord Nelson's morals. You must leave me my more homely idols, my lord. I believe them to have the welfare of simple folk more truly at heart than ever had your gilded heroes."

"Horse, foot and guns!" said the Earl, lost in admiration. "You have rolled me up completely, Miss Kirkley. I can only be grateful that you spared me your views on Lord Byron's morals, which would undoubtedly have made me blush for my sex. I will acknowledge defeat, and your right to choose your own heroes. Even, since you insist, your right to reject a mere smattering of Italian," he added wickedly, with straight face and dancing eyes. "You shall learn the language thoroughly, as you wished."

Elizabeth could not recall having expressed any such desire, but his lordship swept on, leaving her no time to enter an objection.

"And while it grieves me to disappoint your expectations, I do not, in this instance, propose to resort to blackmail. It is tedious, you understand, to repeat oneself, and with all the other arts of villainy at my command your grandmother and aunt may rest secure. This time I shall try bribery."

She could not help being intrigued. "What bribe will you offer, my lord?"

"One that you will find irresistible, and a compliment to boot. I prefer to practise my villainous arts on the grand scale. In return for your promise to attend your dancing lessons regularly, to submit to Miss Trenchard's direction of your general studies, and in particular," with a rueful grimace for the memory of several painful evenings, "to pay careful attention when she instructs you in the rules of card games, I will make you free of my stables. And that, my child, is a compliment which has never been offered to anyone, male or female, until now."

When Hanson had shown her the horses soon after her arrival, she had indulged a wistful hope that she might occasionally be permitted to ride some of these high-bred beauties. To be given the right to choose any one of them whenever she pleased was beyond her wildest imaginings, and it was hard to contain her delight within decorous bounds. The bribe was magnificent—irresistible, as he had forecast—and for so simple a promise, yet she did not wish to give her opponent the satisfaction of knowing how accurately he had gauged her tastes.

There was an amused twinkle in the grey eyes that watched her more closely than she knew. It was not difficult to guess the trend of her thoughts. While she still sought for words in which to express thanks that would seem adequate without sounding fulsome, he went on quietly, "And one thing more. You have been accustomed to a certain degree of freedom, and will, I fear, find it irksome to submit to the constant attendance of a maid or groom whenever you wish to set foot out of doors. Well—I am not quite the tyrant you choose to believe me. On this head at least I have some sympathy with your feelings. Take your groom at first, until you have learned your way about. When you have done so you have my permission to go alone within the boundaries of my land, provided that you always leave word as to the direction in which you have ridden out. And that is merely a necessary precaution in case of accident."

It was more than generous. In a life that seemed suddenly hedged about with a hundred petty restrictions, a blessed interval of privacy and freedom would be doubly precious. The formal phrases she had thought to utter seemed mean and petty in the face of so royal a gesture, and Elizabeth abandoned them, thanking him with a simple sincerity that was pleasant in his ears.

"And I will do my best to keep my share of the bargain," she ended solemnly, as he held the library door open for her, and then, with the glimmering of a smile, "At least I can promise industry, if not enthusiasm."

The Earl laughed, and tapped her soft cheek with one finger. "My dutiful ward!" he mocked lightly. "But I have no fear of your becoming too submissive, Miss Kirkley. Confess now! Do you not enjoy our wordy warfare, and long to annihilate me completely?"

Elizabeth choked on a breath in her surprise, but recovered quickly to retort, "I will confess that I had not expected such perspicacity in you, my lord."

He flung up one hand in laughing despair at her readiness to resume battle. "Content yourself with a tactical victory, my child. When I am reduced to using bribery to attain my ends, I am tacitly conceding defeat."

"And I may really ride any of your horses? And drive them, too?" she added hopefully.

"Trust a woman to wring the last ounce out of a bargain! No. You will not drive my horses—not, at least, until I have had an opportunity to judge for myself how well you can handle the ribbons," he replied, and smiled again to see disappointment quickly succeeded by delighted anticipation on that ingenuous countenance. "You will not of course be wishing to ride Old Warrior, but lest he should feel himself neglected, it would be a kindness in you to give him a word in passing. And when all your duties and delights are done, you may even choose to visit this ogre's den of mine. No"—with gentle malice, as he saw the flicker of dismay in the blue eyes—"no cause for anxiety. I was not proposing to receive you in person. I am rarely here after noon. But you will find many of the books that you seem to prefer on these shelves. Bentham's *Introduction to the Principles of Morals and Legislation* is in the corner there, also several copies of the *Westminster Review*, if you care to glance at that. Only do not give me away to my sister, who would be bound to deprecate such blue-stocking tendencies and give me a tremendous scold for encouraging them."

He did not wait for a reply but closed the door on her, having, as usual, had the last word. His shoulders shook with inward laughter as he moved expectantly to the window. Elizabeth was hurrying stableward as he had guessed she would do. He smiled at the occasional impatient little skip into which eagerness betrayed her, and for quite five minutes after she had disappeared from view he remained gazing absently at the parched lawns, the little smile on his mouth for the memory of the brief comical interlude, before he turned again to his work.

Chapter Five

Elizabeth closed the door of the ballroom with care, and looked about her warily. The library door was fast shut. Heaven send that the Earl was too engrossed in business to notice that this morning the pianoforte was silent. Not that she was really playing truant—not after giving her word. It was M. d'Aubiac himself who had suggested that the lesson should be postponed. It was just that she did not want to be delayed by having to explain matters when the morning freshness was beckoning her out to ride. On soft slippered feet she stole past the dangerous vicinity to the promise of escape held out by the main staircase, but even as she gathered her skirts for the ascent a deep familiar voice bade her a polite good morning and the Earl strolled towards her from the direction of the conservatory, settling a rosy azalea carefully into his button-hole, his cool gaze sweeping her from top to toe with that air of calm appraisal that always aroused her to fury.

"Quite charming, if I may be permitted to say so," he offered gravely, having employed his glass for a more detailed study of her delicate lavender-blue gown. "My sister is to be congratulated on her excellent taste."

"For once, my lord, you are sadly at fault," retorted Elizabeth, "for I chose this gown myself, quite against Lady Maria's advice. *Her* choice was a dull yellow, which nothing would have persuaded me to wear."

There was an appreciative gleam in the grey eyes. "Perhaps she is rather to be congratulated on her masterly strategy," he submitted suavely. "She seems to have found the easiest method of guiding your tastes even so early in your acquaintance."

Elizabeth's chin went up in immediate response to this base insinuation, but before she could utter the impetuous retort that sprang to her lips, the Earl was attacking from another quarter.

"Has M. d'Aubiac been detained this morning? Surely it is the hour for your dancing lesson?"

It was quite maddening to be treated as though she were a naughty schoolgirl. The Earl could not have failed to notice her stealthy retreat, and she was well aware that she must have presented the very image of guilt.

Why could not the obnoxious creature have been safely installed in the library, as he usually was at this hour?

"Miss Trenchard has the migraine this morning," she said stiffly, hating the necessity of making excuses, even though they were true. "M. d'Aubiac thought it better to postpone the lesson, since he could not partner me and play the music at one and the same time."

"I am exceedingly sorry to hear of Miss Trenchard's indisposition," said the Earl kindly. "Tell me—has M. d'Aubiac already left the house?"

Elizabeth thought not. The gentle old man would probably linger over the glass of Madeira and the biscuit that were his chosen refreshment before returning to his quiet lodging.

"Then you need not forego your lesson," said her guardian pleasantly. "M. d'Aubiac shall play for us, and I will undertake to guide your steps to the best of my ability. If you will so far honour me, of course," and he bowed politely and offered his arm to escort her back to the ballroom.

Elizabeth had early succumbed to the dreamy charm of the courteous old Frenchman who was her dancing tutor. She suspected that he stood in sore need of the fee that he earned by teaching her, and did her best to make his task as light as possible. Before long she was enjoying the lessons for their own sake, discovering in herself a natural aptitude for the Terpsichorean art. Moreover, M. d'Aubiac did not confine himself to the teaching of mere steps and figures, but expected his pupil to engage in polite conversation with her partner while performing the most complicated evolutions with negligent grace. His talk gave her a glimpse of a lost world, a world where all was smoothly cushioned and comfortable for the wealthy and the well-born, for he was a child of pre-Revolution France. It was a world that seemed artificial and incomprehensible to Elizabeth. She questioned him eagerly about the changes that the Revolution had brought to the oppressed peasantry. M. d'Aubiac shook his silver head. He was too old to care greatly for such matters. She would do better to discuss them with her guardian, who was known to concern himself deeply with the welfare of his dependents.

He rose now to greet his pupil and her escort with such genuine pleasure that Elizabeth could only wonder again at the perversity of men. It was quite clear that this kindly old man shared Timothy's predilection for the Earl's society, and when their errand was explained he was wholly delighted to have an opportunity of displaying his pupil's progress to his patron.

He was to be disappointed. All Elizabeth's natural grace seemed to have deserted her. She moved as stiffly as any puppet, forgot her steps and once actually stumbled, while her replies to the Earl's courteous remarks were monosyllabic. Poor M. d'Aubiac could not understand it. Never had the child displayed such gaucherie, even at her first lesson. He brought the figure to an end and humbly awaited the caustic comment that its performance merited.

"I find it surprisingly difficult," said the Earl in an apologetic tone, "to perform a figure meant for four when there are only two of us. I wonder, M. d'Aubiac, have you by any fortunate chance taught Miss Kirkley to waltz?"

"Yes, indeed," exclaimed the old man eagerly, "and she shows marked proficiency."

"Then will you consent to try the steps with me, Miss Kirkley?"

Elizabeth was reluctant, flushed with shame over her abysmal performance, yet anxious to redeem her teacher's credit. She curtsied a silent consent, fearful lest her voice should break and betray her distress, and permitted the Earl to take her in his hold while M. d'Aubiac played the lilting rhythm, softly at first as he watched the girl's timidly correct steps and then with increasing verve as he saw her respond to the seduction of the music and her partner's firm guidance.

The Earl was an excellent dancer, as behoved an officer who had served under Lord Wellington. Waltzing with him was quite different from waltzing with Miss Trenchard, or even with M. d'Aubiac. It was strangely pleasurable to relax and allow the man and the music to take command. When the dance came to an end Elizabeth looked up at her guardian and for the first time in their acquaintance smiled at him with genuine warmth. Nor did she need her teacher's prompting. "Thank you, my lord, that was most enjoyable," she said, rather shyly, but with clear sincerity.

His face was inscrutable as ever. He did not return her smile, rather studying her face as though trying to identify a resemblance dimly perceived. Then he said, almost absently, "You are very like your father when you smile, Miss Kirkley," and as he relaxed his hold and offered his arm to escort her back to M. d'Aubiac at the pianoforte, added quietly, "It was a great pleasure to me, too. I do not know when I have enjoyed a waltz so much. Your pupil is a credit to you, Monsieur. When my nephew arrives we must invite some of our young neighbours for one or two informal dances. In that way Miss Kirkley may become at much at home in the quadrilles and the country dances as she is in the waltz. And she waltzes beautifully."

It actually seemed possible that the erstwhile antagonists might subscribe to a truce, but unfortunately this promising situation was interrupted by the entry of the butler.

"Mr Christison has called, my lord, and is very urgent to speak with you. I have shown him into the library."

"Thank you, Harrison. Say that I will be with him almost at once. Miss Kirkley, shall you be riding out this afternoon?"

Elizabeth admitted that this was her intention.

"Then I wish that you will ride out by the South Lodge and enquire if there is anything that we may do for Sarah. John tells me that she is growing very feeble."

Though perfectly willing to lend her assistance, Elizabeth was a little surprised at the request. She had met old Sarah only once, and it seemed to her unlikely that the crabbed ancient would confide in a stranger. She could not help feeling that Lady Hester would have been a more suitable messenger. However, she made no demur, and the Earl went off to confer with his anxious neighbour.

Mr Christison's normal good-tempered expression was under a cloud this morning. He looked hot and harassed, and upon the Earl's entry he burst into speech without wasting time on commonplace courtesies.

"That noddy of yours has been up to his tricks again, Anderley. He was for opening the sluices last night, and if I'd not had a man on guard, the lot would have gone. You'll have to do something about him or there'll be bad trouble. The men won't stand much more. It's not even as if he were a local lad."

Having unburdened himself of his complaint, his humour seemed to improve. He eyed the Earl's grave countenance with some sympathy, and went on more temperately, "I'm sorry for the man. Don't doubt he was all you say until he took that head wound at Waterloo. But there's no gainsaying he's a menace now and ought to be shut up. If he gets at those sluices my mill must stop, and there's forty men thrown out of employment, and no hope of starting up again until this confounded drought breaks. I've doubled the guard on the dam and, believe me, if they catch him again they'll not be gentle."

"Was there violence last night?"

"Naught to speak of. Just a bit of a turn up. He went off quiet enough when he saw it was no good, but he was muttering threats about not being done with them yet, along with a lot of stuff about streams of living water on the thirsty land."

"Poor devil!" said the Earl soberly. "I'll get him away as soon as I can, but he'll have to be watched. John can manage him better than most, but I can't spare John for a day or so. There's this murderous business of culling the deer to be got over with, and he's the best marksman on the place. Can you manage to guard your sluices till I've dealt with that? We're making a start today, and you can imagine we'll try to make short work of it. Then I'll get John to take poor Garrett over to Coldstone. If he could be settled there it is isolated enough to solve several problems."

Mr Christison nodded. "Ye're too soft-hearted, Anderley," he grunted. "Time you learned you can't carry all the world on your shoulders, even if they did serve in your old regiment. As for the deer—well—it's a damnable business, but a quick clean death is better than dying of thirst, and God knows there's little enough water for human beings, let alone the brute beasts. Who's doing the job?"

"Myself, with John and Bassett," said the Earl curtly.

"Well, thank God I'm a plain mill owner with no deer park to worry about. What's more I'm but a moderate shot at best, so I can't offer to help you—and I'm thankful for that, too," he ended with characteristic bluntness.

The Earl's grim expression relaxed. "You're an old fraud, Hector," he said, shaking his friend gently by the shoulder. "*You* to accuse *me* of being soft-hearted. Who's been keeping the weavers on full wages, and they working no more than half time?"

Mr Christison went purple with embarrassment as one discovered in some shameful act, and spluttered something incoherent about not wanting to lose good workers to some rival employer.

"Just so," agreed the Earl innocently. "We all know you're a hard-headed North-countryman, squeezing the last ounce out of your men. Don't talk to me about my old soldiers, you double-dyed deceiver! Be off to your beloved looms, and leave me to my bloody massacre."

Chapter Six

Elizabeth set about her mission early. She had been distinctly shaken by the mingled emotions aroused in the morning's encounter. For once, she discovered, she was not detesting her guardian quite so thoroughly as usual. He had shown himself considerate of her dear M. d'Aubiac, refraining from the scathing comment that her performance had certainly merited. As for the waltz that had followed, she found herself strangely reluctant to dwell on the response that it had evoked in her. It was not surprising, she decided, that careful mamas frowned upon the dance.

She wandered restlessly through the pleasant apartments that had been set aside for her use. A peep into Miss Trenchard's room showed that lady to be deeply asleep. She felt disinclined for reading or for needlework, and glanced with contempt at the sketch of the fountain that Mary had persuaded her to begin. She felt stifled by the comfort that enveloped her, thirsted for freedom, and decided to take her ride now, finish her errand, and then spend a long afternoon in leisurely exploration of this new countryside. Her freedom to do so brought her guardian to mind once more, and as she rang for her maid she dwelt for a moment or two on the queer quirks of the man. As Edith helped her to change her pretty gown for riding dress, she was wondering how one so stern and hard could have foreseen and understood her need for an occasional escape from her silken fetters.

For there was no gainsaying that in a life where every waking moment seemed to have its carefully planned and supervised occupation, one longed for privacy and independence. How had the Earl known that this would be her need? And how had he known that young Edith, barely seventeen and quite overwhelmed by her good fortune in being chosen to serve Miss Kirkley, was just the kind of handmaid she needed? A practised and fashionable dresser would have petrified her—who had never known any other ministrations than those of her nurse. As it was, she and Edith were learning together, and getting a good deal of innocent fun in the process.

Reluctantly she was beginning to concede that she might have been a little mistaken in her first judgement of her guardian. Harsh and overbearing he could certainly be when his will was crossed, but it seemed that he could also be kind if one were submissive. It was a pity that Elizabeth Hamerton, who still could not accustom herself to being Elizabeth Kirkley, was not of a submissive disposition.

She dimpled at the thought, and assuring the solicitous Edith that she was not in the least hungry and would not stay for a luncheon, went off to the stables.

She stopped, as usual, for a word with Old Warrior. The last of the Earl's chargers, he was living out his old age in well-earned luxury. That was another queer facet of his lordship's character, she thought, as the great tall fellow bowed his head and snuffed lovingly at her neck. How could a man be so callous in his dealings with defenceless women, and yet care that a horse's feelings should not be hurt just because he was old and useless? Could the threats that he had used at their first meeting to ensure her obedience have been no more than a bluff? She was beginning to think that this might well be the truth of the matter. Not that it lessened her indignation, since she and her family, in their simplicity, had been completely taken in.

The mare she was riding this morning was a gentle creature with a lovely smooth action but a rather nervous disposition. A brisk canter down the grass ride that would bring her out at the South Lodge soon dispelled the growing tendency to brood over the idiosyncrasies of her guardian, but arrived at her destination she suffered a check. A middle-aged woman, a stranger to her, was standing in the gateway waving farewell to the occupants of a farm cart which was trundling away down the road, and bundled up in a chair set in the body of the cart was the old dame she had come to visit. The woman turned to bob a curtsy as she drew the mare to a halt, and bade her a smiling good-day.

"I came to see Sarah," explained Elizabeth rather shyly. "His lordship wished me to enquire if there was anything she needed."

"Why, thank you, Miss. 'Twas kind in you to put yourself to the trouble. But me and George, we've persuaded her to go to Nancy's—that's me sister, Miss. I'm Sarah's youngest daughter, Kate, but she wouldn't come to me, knowing I'm throng with the childer. Nancy'll see to her, and George and me have promised to keep the lodge redded up and look after

John. So she's gone off content enough. But you'll be sure and thank his lordship kindly, won't you, Miss?"

Having declined offers of hospitality ranging from elder-flower wine to a slice of ginger cake, Elizabeth was free to pursue her own fancy. She turned the mare back along the verge of the drive, deciding on a wide circuit that would take her beyond the cultivated lands to the open moor that bordered the north-western limits of the Anderley estate like some purple-bronze ocean. The air was fresher on those barren heights, and tangy with wild thyme. She held the mare to a gentle trot, for the going was treacherous in places, and one must keep a wary eye for hidden rabbit holes.

She viewed with lively interest each new aspect that opened before her critical gaze. In a normal season, she decided, Anderley must be very lovely. Even in conditions of severe drought it still held a muted charm derived of winding paths, ever-changing levels, and glimpses of distant hills. If only the dried-out streams and rivulets had been alive with chuckling water, the herbage soft and green instead of the burned and dusty brown! That poor fourth Earl who had devoted all his energies to the laying out of the grounds must surely be haunting the vicinity, his sad ghost wringing mournful hands over the drooping trees, their leaves already yellowing as though autumn were come.

An unusual sound assailed her ears, and the mare flinched and tossed her head. Elizabeth soothed the high-strung creature with hand and voice. But surely that had been a rifle shot, and what could anyone be shooting at this season? Probably a keeper after vermin, she was thinking, when two shots range out in close succession, so startling the mare that she tried to bolt. All Elizabeth's skill was needed to bring the terrified animal under control, a task rendered all the more difficult by the reports of several more shots at irregular intervals. Not until she turned aside into a sheltered dell whose high banks muffled the sounds did she succeed in quieting her sweating, shivering mount. By that time she was both annoyed and curious, and determined to find out what was going on. She slid down from the saddle, trusting to luck to find a convenient rock or tree stump to help her mount again.

Having secured the mare, she retraced her steps and stood listening for a moment until the sound of more shots gave her direction. Riding habit and boots were not very suited to a woodland walk, and brambles snatching at her skirts as she struggled up the steeply rising path did nothing to cool her temper. Then, as she reached the little crest and looked down into the hollow below, anger was swamped in a passion of horror and pity. The floor of the hollow seemed to be littered with bodies—a score and more. Deer—the pretty, gentle creatures whose tameness had so surprised her, until Lady Hester had explained that they were accustomed to being fed in the hard winters.

With no thought in her mind but that this cruel slaughter must be stopped at once, she snatched up her hampering skirts and began to run down the path, slipping and stumbling on the rocks and heedless of danger to herself. Another shot cracked out from a clump of bushes where some marksman was concealed. There was a sudden fierce shout from close beside her. Startled, she slipped once more, lost her balance, and subsided into a huddled heap, pain shooting through a wrenched ankle.

Before she could struggle to her feet again, strong hands were gripping her shoulders and a well-known voice was demanding urgently, "You're not hit? It was only a tumble?" Still breathless, she shook her head, whereupon the voice snapped, on quite a different note, "Then what in God's name possessed you to run out under the guns, you little fool?"

She had managed to pull herself up, but was forced to cling to his arm since her ankle would not support her weight. From this ignominious position she glared up at the Earl's furious face.

"Someone had to stop you, you murderous brute! You deserve shooting yourself—except it's too merciful. A fine afternoon's sport you have had, to be sure. Could you not find anything more helpless and defenceless for the exercise of your skill?"

The anger faded from the Earl's face as he looked down at her flushed cheeks and quivering lips. The blue eyes were bright with tears. The tongue-lashing he heeded not at all.

"John!" he called crisply over his shoulder. The tall groom was already coming up at a run, the stockier Bassett following more slowly. "Get down to the house and ask them to send the light chaise round to Bassett's cottage. Miss Kirkley has hurt her foot." Then, to the girl, "Where did you leave your horse?"

She jerked her head in the direction of the woods, but having exhausted her first rage, could not bring herself to speak to him.

"See to it, will you, Bassett," said the Earl casually, and bent with cool impersonality to lift her, adding to the gamekeeper, "I'll carry Miss Kirkley to your cottage. Lucy can attend to her foot."

A raging Elizabeth protested furiously that she was perfectly well able to walk and would much prefer to do so.

"Don't be ridiculous," said the Earl calmly. "You could not even stand unsupported. It is no distance to Bassett's cottage, and though I may be ancient I am not yet quite decrepit." And settling her more securely in his hold he strode along the narrow path.

Elizabeth glanced helplessly at the strong brown hands that were holding her so easily. There was a smear of blood across the back of one of them.

"My objections are prompted less by consideration for your age and decrepitude than by distaste for having you touch me," she informed him with as much dignity as her absurd position permitted, and pointed to the blood on his hand.

He looked—and laughed. "You can spare the melodrama. It's my own. And shed in your behalf, if we must have heroics. I tore it on the briars when I picked you up. Surely you are aware that the slaughter of defenceless deer is not only a safe sport but a clean one? There is no need to soil one's hands with their blood. However, since this is Bassett's cottage, I will release you from my unhallowed grasp." And bending his tall head to the low lintel he carried her into the cottage, set her down with scant ceremony on a bench beside the window, and then walked through into the kitchen shouting for Lucy.

Lucy must have been outside in the garden, for several minutes elapsed before the sound of voices in the adjoining room announced her presence. Elizabeth was grateful for the brief respite. Her ankle was throbbing painfully, she felt rather sick, and viewed with apprehension the prospect of having her boot removed. She studied Lucy with painful concentration, trying to fix her thoughts on anything that might offer distraction from her physical discomfort. The girl was slim and dark and young, probably a year or so younger than she was herself. She smiled at Elizabeth and took her hand in a comforting clasp as the Earl knelt to remove the boot. The ordeal was not so bad as she had feared. The strong brown hands— cleansed of blood, she noticed inconsequently—were deft and quick. Carefully he peeled away the tough fabric and Lucy gave a sympathetic little whimper of pity at the swelling and discolouration that showed even through the stocking.

"It will soon feel better, Miss," she said encouragingly.

The Earl nodded agreement. "Yes. Nothing broken. Cold water first, then hot, Lucy. Keep changing from one to the other. And perhaps a hot drink," he added thoughtfully, viewing the tightly set composure of the sufferer's mouth. "Tea, if you have it—or one of your cordials." He rose from his knees and strolled out of the room.

Lucy bustled about with bowls and towels and a kettle of hot water. Elizabeth submitted thankfully to her competent ministrations, and as the pain in her ankle began to subside, curiosity stirred. For Lucy was an unusual sort of girl to find in a gamekeeper's cottage. Though she had a northcountry brogue, her speech was clear and correct. Her manners were pleasant, neither forward nor shy, and her dress was becoming and of excellent quality—such, indeed, as Elizabeth Hamerton might well have worn herself. Altogether a surprising creature to find in this tiny isolated cottage.

The bathing done, and the injured foot supported on a cushion on a stool, Lucy brought out a bottle of blackcurrant cordial, apologising that she had no tea to offer, but father did not care for it and it was not worth the bother and expense just for herself. While she warmed the cordial with a watchful eye on Elizabeth's white face, she chattered easily about such homely matters as the making of cordials and preserves and the problems of housekeeping in this remote dale.

"And everything so much more troublesome now, with the drought," she went on, carrying the cup to Elizabeth's side. "'Tis great good fortune that our spring has not dried up, for it is close on two miles to the village, and that's a good step to be carrying every drop of water. I was hearing that they've put a guard on the village pump for fear of water thieves."

Elizabeth, reviving to the hot drink, began to feel ashamed of her own ignorance. Lapped in the comfort of Anderley and wholly absorbed in trying to adjust herself to her new situation, she had given no thought to how others were faring in this time of general hardship.

"I had not understood that things were quite so bad," she admitted. "Is water so scarce that people are actually stealing it?"

Lucy looked astonished. "Why yes, Miss—and much ill feeling about, what with the hay crop all burned up and the price of fodder so high. If it were not for Lord Anderley remitting the rents, not to mention sending water carts round the hamlets where there is greatest need, and Mr Christison at the mill paying full wages all along, there's many would be in sore straits. And now his lordship having to kill off all those poor trusting creatures that were dying of thirst because he dare not give them the water that must be saved for the villages and the farm stock. My father says he was sorely grieved to do it, but done it must be, and he'd handle the horrid business himself rather than put it on to anyone else. Only father and Mr Hanson are such good shots you see—with them he could count on it that the poor things wouldn't suffer—so he permitted them to help him."

The hot blood dyed Elizabeth's pale face scarlet. One hand flew to her mouth. "Oh dear!" she said weakly. "And I called him a murdering brute! But, Lucy—I didn't understand. I thought—I thought they were shooting for pleasure."

The enormity of the error shattered Lucy's easy composure. Quite frankly she gaped. Then she drew a deep breath, and with careful restraint began to explain to Elizabeth just how mistaken she had been. A subdued Elizabeth listened meekly to yet another ardent champion of his lordship, too crushed by her own crass blunder to defend herself. Lucy had not nearly reached the end of her panegyric when the sound of wheels on the roughly surfaced track announced the arrival of the chaise to carry the casualty back to Anderley.

She should have been thankful that the Earl seemed to have vanished into the landscape, for his presence would have called for an immediate and abject apology, and though it was undoubtedly his due, she burned with shame at the prospect. John lifted her gently and carefully and established her as comfortably as possible in the chaise with her foot supported along the seat. Lucy tenderly laid the remains of the dissected boot on the floor beside her. There were promises of another visit and all the gentle fuss and flutter of farewell.

So why should she feel neglected and bereft?

Chapter Seven

The injured ankle kept Elizabeth a prisoner in her own room for two days. Lady Hester fussed over her delightedly, even going so far as to bring one of her beloved King Charles spaniels to bear the sufferer company and keep her amused with his mischievous tricks. Mary seized the opportunity to read reams of poetry to her, in the vain hope of overcoming her unfashionable aversion to this form of literary art. She was surrounded by kindness and cosetted to death—and felt more than ever restless and stifled as well as guiltily ungrateful.

Lady Hester had always been dubious about the practice of riding alone, and felt that her brother had been wrong to allow it in the first place. She could not be expected to refrain from pointing out that events had justified her expectations. Nor did she approve of his lordship's action in taking the girl to Bassett's cottage. "Most unsuitable," she declared, with unusual severity for one of her gentle disposition. "It would have been far better to bring you straight home." When Elizabeth questioned her about Lucy Bassett she learned that Lucy had been in service, had in fact been so fortunate as to obtain a post with Lady Maria, but had proved to be quite unsuitable. Lucy, said Lady Hester severely, had ideas much above her station. Why, she had actually begged Lady Maria to allow her to attend a Sunday school so that she might learn to read, perhaps even to write! "Quite impossible, of course. I would not for the world have had Richard take you there. But he is always so careless of public opinion."

To Elizabeth, who could see nothing in the least wicked or revolutionary in Lucy's innocent ambitions, this sweeping condemnation was incomprehensible. But since Lady Hester was obviously reluctant to discuss the Bassetts further, she obligingly turned the conversation to the promised visit of Timothy Elsford and the Earl's suggestion of dancing parties. Lady Hester was delighted. It was so long since they had entertained any but shooting parties. How pleasant it would be to have young people about the place. She began at once to make lists of all those who might or must be invited, and Lucy Bassett's peccadilloes were happily forgotten.

In her rare intervals of solitude Elizabeth faced the need of apologising to her guardian. She could not remember exactly what terms of censure she had used in her disgust and rage, but they had probably been as unbecoming to her as they were unjust to him. Her cheeks burned anew as she pictured how he would sneer at her ignorance. No. That was unjust too. He never sneered. But his patient tolerance was almost as bad. He made one feel so pitifully young and inadequate. Elizabeth, who at twenty-three considered herself perfectly capable of conducting her own affairs, felt that she could very well do without his management. Nevertheless there was no evading the fact that she had done him a grave injustice and must confess her fault. Except that she had no wish to limp into the library leaning on a stick—a tacit appeal for pity—she would be been done with the odious necessity already. So she was divided between gratitude and apprehension when Dr Hartwell said she might emerge from the seclusion of her room and resume her usual habits so long as she rested the weak ankle frequently. She was craven enough to take breakfast in bed—she really could not face him publicly over the breakfast table—but as soon as that was done she rang for Edith and achieved her toilet with unusual expedition. Then there could be no more putting off, and after a stiff and awkward descent of the main staircase she stood hesitating before the library door.

Her first knock sounded so timid and tentative in her own ears that she promptly followed it up with a much more aggressive assault, and then started back in foolish alarm when the Earl's calm voice bade her come in. Oh dear! How wonderful it would have been to sweep into the room with her most dignified air, express her regrets in the polished phrases she had so carefully rehearsed and be done with the whole affair. Instead she must make her halting entry upon what seemed to be at least an acre of gleaming oaken floor, the Earl, at his writing table, as remote and unapproachable as any monarch.

That impression at least was banished almost as soon as it formed, for at sight of her he had sprung to his feet and crossed that treacherous expanse in a few swift strides to lend her the support of his arm, enquiring the while if she was really well enough to be about so soon.

"Yes indeed, my lord," she assured him earnestly. "I had to come as soon as possible. I came—I came—" frantically she searched her memory for those painstakingly acquired phrases—"to express my regret for having so misjudged your actions. I am truly sorry—"

She got no further. He was half smiling and shaking his head as he laid a finger lightly across her lips. "Please, Miss Kirkley! The fault was quite my own. There is no need to pour coals of fire. I should have admitted you into my confidence and explained the situation instead of sending you off on a foolish errand that I hoped would spare you the horrid knowledge of my necessity. I might then have earned your sympathy rather than your detestation. Indeed it is for *me* to beg *your* pardon."

So generous a reception wholly disarmed Elizabeth. She quite forgot that his was her tyrannical guardian and poured out her sympathy over his predicament in a warm, impulsive way that she had not permitted herself since she had been reft from her home. From the sorry business of the deer they passed naturally enough to other aspects of the water shortage, the Earl showing her a chart on which the daily state of all the springs and wells had been recorded and explaining how Mr Christison's mill was working short time to conserve the water left in the mill pool, releasing just sufficient each day to serve the needs of the valley farms. Before either of them quite knew it they were deep in discussion of the responsibilities of landowners and employers of labour, and it was not until the library clock struck twelve that Elizabeth awoke to the realisation that the morning had fled and that she had kept the Earl from whatever task had been engaging him upon her arrival. She got up, blushing and apologising, and the Earl assured her that only some very dull correspondence had been neglected, and that could be dealt with at any time.

Even after he had closed the door behind her he did not at once apply himself to the task, but sat for a long time deep in thought, turning the pen abstractedly between his fingers. Then, with a shrug and a wry little grimace, he pulled forward a fresh sheet of notepaper and began a new letter. It was addressed to his nephew Timothy, and it suggested that, if his engagements permitted, Timothy should put forward the date of his arrival at Anderley.

The damaged ankle took its time to mend, and the days of enforced physical idleness seemed endless. She scarcely set eyes on the Earl except at dinner, and then he appeared unusually silent and withdrawn. She would have welcomed the distraction of one of their typical arguments. Even better would have been such good talk as they had shared that morning in the library. Lady Hester and Mary were sweet and considerate, but their interests were purely feminine. Elizabeth, having discovered the exhilaration of serious masculine talk, was eager for more. She was even guilty of deliberately varying the time of her appearance at breakfast in the hope of a chance encounter, but her luck was quite out and she had to make do with Lady Hester's gentle vapourings or the high moral tone of Mary's serious discourse. Had she but known it her ill-luck was a blessing in disguise, since of all things the Earl detested being obliged to make conversation over the breakfast table, a social necessity that he described as being positively barbarous. In happy ignorance of this common male foible, she continued to regret his absence. There was not even dear M. d'Aubiac to talk to, for of necessity the dancing lessons had been discontinued until such time as her ankle was better.

"I really am becoming the horridest creature," she thought ruefully, when, at long last, she was able to make good her escape and the mare was trotting down the avenue. "Being a lady of leisure doesn't suit me at all. There just isn't enough to do, and so I snap and snarl at kind people who think I should do even less."

In this she was doing herself less than justice, for she had been perfectly polite, reassuring Lady Hester, who had protested that it was much too soon for her to be riding, and wouldn't she at least take a groom? Mary's face of sober disapproval she had carefully ignored. Mary, she had discovered, while outwardly admiring, secretly regarded the Earl's horses in much the same light that a medieval damsel viewed the dragon in the old romances—as a necessary but most uncomfortable appurtenance to the background of a man of quality. She did, however, suffer a genuine qualm of conscience at the realisation that in the fuss over her departure she had quite forgotten the Earl's order that she should leave word in which direction she proposed to ride out. She had felt that Lady Hester's disapproval of the outing would only be strengthened by the knowledge that her intention was to visit Lucy Bassett. She *had* meant to leave word at the stables, but with John unaccountably absent, no one else had thought to ask her where she was bound, and she herself had quite forgotten the oversight until now. She must just hope that no mishap would befall her today, for to go back now would only mean more fuss and delay, and after a week's imprisonment the taste of freedom was sweet. She rode on.

The cottage had quite a welcoming air as she approached it, for the front door was standing open, but there was no answer to her knock. She could scarcely walk in, calling for Lucy, as the Earl had done, but in view of the open door there must surely be someone about the place. After a brief hesitation she rode round to the back of the building. Ah! There was Lucy, busily engaged in spreading linen over some low-growing bushes, and equally busy with her was a fair-haired mite of perhaps three or four years old, seriously intent on spreading her doll's garments on the greensward in careful imitation.

Lucy swung round at the sound of hoofs, said something in low tones to the little girl, and then came quietly towards Elizabeth. The child stayed where she was, gazing round-eyed at the visitor.

"Good morning, Miss Kirkley," said Lucy composedly. "I hope your ankle is quite well again. Will you not come indoors and rest awhile? It is full soon for you to be riding all this way after such a nasty fall. We can turn the mare into the croft here," and she indicated a tiny enclosure which was already occupied by a cow and some hens.

Elizabeth came down from the saddle willingly enough. Truth to tell, she would be glad of a brief rest, having rather overestimated her capabilities, but she declined the offer of refreshment and said that she would rather sit a while on the low wall that enclosed the garden, so that she need not hinder Lucy's work. They could talk just as well in the open air. Lucy's hesitation was patent, but she made no objection and held open the gate for the visitor to pass through. The little girl came slowly towards them.

"This is Mally," said Lucy gently. "Make your curtsy to the lady, Mally."

The child wobbled an unsteady little bob, and continued to stare solemnly at Elizabeth, one small pink thumb eventually finding its way into her mouth to her obvious comfort.

"She is not much used to company," said Lucy excusingly. "Not many visitors find their way so far from the village." She went on with her work, talking easily enough of the difficulty of keeping linen a good colour now that she could no longer use the stream for rinsing. The little girl had picked up her doll and was crooning a tuneless lullaby as she rocked it in her arms. All seemed simple and natural enough. Yet Elizabeth was aware of some sort of constraint in the atmosphere. She could not help wondering who the child was. Hardly a neighbour's child, so far from any other habitation, yet she had certainly understood that Bassett was a widower with just one unmarried daughter who kept house for him. There were other puzzles too. The child's clothes were of the finest quality, the doll she cuddled an expensive one. There was certainly no lack of money in this humble home.

Elizabeth had liked Lucy at their first meeting, and had come today with no other motive than to thank the girl for her kindness. She had no wish to pry into Lucy's affairs and tried to stifle her natural curiosity, yet her gaze would keep wandering to Mally's fair head, so different from Lucy's gipsy-dark good looks. The child had an elusive likeness to someone she had met, but she could not quite pin it down. At this point Mally solved one problem for her by tumbling down and setting up an immediate wail for 'Mammy'. Luckily Elizabeth had time to bring her features under control while Lucy gently rubbed the bump 'to make it better', and dried the tears on the rosy cheeks, for the shock was considerable. Here, of course, was the real reason why Lady Hester had so disapproved of her introduction to Lucy.

She felt deeply sorry for the girl, and instantly comprehensive of the wary defensive look on her face as she knelt beside the child, holding her close in the circle of her arm, the two of them together against the world.

"Would Mally like a ride?" she asked gently. "I could take her up in front of me. Or you could hold her in the saddle while I walk the mare."

Lucy's eyes shone with a gratitude that was not for the proffered treat. "Oh! You are kind, truly kind," she said huskily. "But I think she would be frightened. Perhaps I could hold her up to stroke the mare's neck. That would be excitement enough. She is only a baby yet."

The pathetically eager gratitude was very touching. On a sudden warm impulse Elizabeth said, "Lady Hester was telling me that you dearly wished to learn to read. I wondered if perhaps I could help you."

There was the shine of tears in the dark eyes as the girl shook her head. "It is too late. I have so little time now, with Mally to care for. And though my father is very kind to me, he would not like it. He will not have me put myself forward in any way. But Mally shall learn when she is old enough," she finished fiercely, and then, diffidently, "Perhaps, sometimes, Miss Kirkley, if you are riding this way, you will stop for a word or two? It can be very lonely here. And Mally and I can do you no harm."

"That I will certainly do," said Elizabeth firmly. "And if there is any other way in which I may serve you I beg you will let me know. I shall not easily forget your kindness at our first meeting."

Chapter Eight

Lady Hester came down to dinner in disconsolate mood. As the first course was being removed the cause of her plaint was disclosed. "Really, Richard," she said reproachfully, "it is quite too bad. I have gone to a great deal of trouble, making plans for these parties that you promised the child, and I have just remembered that she is in mourning. It is quite your blame for insisting that she wears colours, else I should certainly not have forgotten."

The Earl emerged from a deep abstraction. "Parties, Hester?" he said vaguely. "It is scarcely the time to be giving parties with so much distress about. Do you really think you should?"

"Elizabeth tells me that you yourself suggested giving one or two informal morning parties for her," persisted Lady Hester. "So far as the poverty in the district is concerned, we should certainly need to take on extra maids to help with the preparations, so it would be quite an act of charity to do so, and, incidentally, with John away so much, we could well employ one or two extra men in the stables. But that is not the point. Would it be proper for us to give even the simplest party under the circumstances?"

Since his sister seemed to be deeply concerned, the Earl obligingly bent his mind to the problem. An evening party, he pronounced, was quite ineligible, but one or two mornings devoted to the practice of the latest dances, under the guidance of M. d'Aubiac, could be counted as educational, and therefore unexceptionable. There could be some form of cold collation to add a touch of modest festivity—his sister would know best what was appropriate.

Lady Hester considered his suggestions doubtfully. "It sounds dreadfully dull," she sighed. "I suppose there could be no objections to my engaging extra musicians? But I daresay you are in the right of it. We must certainly not do anything to prejudice Elizabeth's prospects when she comes out next year," and she smiled at the girl with affectionate benevolence.

"You would do well to defer your parties until after Timothy's arrival," said the Earl helpfully. "He can then act as host, in my behalf."

Elizabeth looked up with a gleam of pleased anticipation that did not escape the speaker. It would be pleasant, she was thinking, to meet Mr Elsford again. But Lady Hester, not to be bamboozled by her brother's nonchalant delegation of his duties, expressed her disapproval.

"Should you not be present yourself, Richard? I am sure there is not the least need for you to join in the dancing," she added kindly, "but our guests will be sadly disappointed if they do not even see you."

Both Maria and Hester, their brother reflected with an inward smile, were apt to forget the twenty odd years that separated them from him. He had never discouraged their peculiar belief that he was of their own generation. Indeed it had seemed to him eminently desirable that Maria, at least, should be prevented from adopting elder sisterly airs. Hester, bred in a gentler mould, had never presumed to order his conduct and accorded him all the respect due to the head of the family, but there were times when her unconscious assumption that he was middle-aged, bordering on elderly, had been mildly irritating. On this occasion he was actually glad of it. It was no part of his plan to further his acquaintance with his attractive ward. Timothy must be allowed a clear field.

He shook his head. "As you have just implied, my dear, I am far too old for such junketings. Besides, my presence would add just that note of formality that we are anxious to avoid. Timothy will do it very well, and there will be no stern martinet present to cast a damper on the proceedings." And though his sister indignantly denied that she had meant any such thing, he only laughed, assured her that she had given him a splendid excuse for crying off, and would not be persuaded. Elizabeth was conscious of a surprisingly keen disappointment. She had looked forward to dancing with her guardian again. It was all the fault of that insidious waltz.

There were few things that Lady Hester enjoyed better than arranging parties, and however modest their scope, everything must be done perfectly for the honour of Anderley. The extent of the 'cold collation' grew daily in magnificence and variety as she thought of new and indispensable delights. Everyone was sure to be hungry after such an energetic morning, and it would be shameful beyond words if her provision was insufficient for healthy young appetites. Then the ballroom must be furbished up, the lustres of the great chandeliers washed and polished, and elegant Chinese screens set across one third of the room's length lest it should seem too vast for so small a party. "For nothing," she assured her fascinated listeners, "is more fatal to the success of *any* party than too much *space*. You can positively *see* the guests wondering why so few are present, and naturally wishing themselves elsewhere."

Elizabeth was left wondering whether the arrival of King George himself could have caused more fuss and excitement. But it was infectious. She felt more gay and light-hearted than at any time since her translation. Her laughter came readily, and she sang softly to herself as she ran Lady Hester's many errands, a change of mood which did not escape the Earl's percipient eye, and upon which he placed his own interpretation. She found time, among her many small preoccupations, to visit the lonely cottage at the head of the dale, and generally contrived to take some small treat for Mally, perhaps a few shining beads to string, or a gaily striped sugar stick. It was pleasant to see how the shy mite now ran to greet her and held up dimpled arms to be lifted and hugged, and Lucy's glance of warm content at her coming was royal welcome. They talked only of surface matters, Elizabeth respecting the girl's reticence. Most of all, of course, they talked of the small Mally, and of her future when she should be old enough to be put to school. Once, in an unguarded moment, Lucy confided that she was saving part of her allowance each quarter to meet the cost of schooling. Elizabeth tacitly ignored the slip, speaking instead of her own schooldays, a subject that Lucy found so fascinating that she never realised how she had betrayed herself.

Riding home, Elizabeth could not help pondering the source of that 'allowance'. Mally's unknown father was obviously a man of means and had at least had sufficient humanity to make provision for the child. But she quite forgot Lucy and her problems when she rode into a stable yard all a-bustle with the signs of new arrival. Could it be that Mr Elsford was come, and sooner than was expected? And even as she swung down from the saddle she heard his boyish laughter and turned to discover him paying off the post boys with a liberality indicated by their wide grins. He had not seen her and she did not stay to greet him, but handed over the mare to Jacky, her own particular groom, and slipped away quietly along the covered way that gave access to a side door.

Her memories of Mr Elsford were warmly grateful, and it was in a mood of happy anticipation that she made her evening toilet. Mr Elsford had never seen her in her new plumage. It would be amusing to watch his reactions to it. She studied her finished reflection in the mirror for so long that Edith grew anxious and asked if she had done aught amiss. Elizabeth reassured the child and dismissed her, then, half ashamed of her own vanity, went back to the mirror.

The girl who looked back at her no longer went hatless out of doors. Her skin was clear and smooth, while her hair had certainly grown silkier from Edith's assiduous brushing. The simple arrangement which was all that the girl could manage was quaint but becoming, swept up to show the pure line of brow and cheek, and framing the slim throat between soft ringlets.

She wished she was not quite so tall—almost as tall as Mr Elsford. It took a man of the Earl's inches to make her feel fragile and feminine. But her figure, she decided, was good, and her gown of soft rose-coloured gauze wickedly enhanced its attractions. She spanned a slender waist with her hands, pointed one toe and swung her skirts to reveal a delicate ankle, then primmed her lips in reproof of her own posturing. How rapidly one's character deteriorated when one led a wholly frivolous and fashionable existence, she thought solemnly, recalling Mary's lectures on the subject, and then laughed at herself, knowing quite well that at the moment she was thoroughly enjoying her own fashionable appearance and looking forward to an evening of pure pleasure.

And for once—for perhaps the first time in her restricted life—the evening fulfilled every expectation. Even the scene seemed to have been set for her, for thanks to her lingering at the mirror she was a little late, and the rest of the party were already gathered in the hall as she came down the staircase. Lady Hester had donned a gown of stiff green silk with elaborately padded hem and voluminous sleeves in honour of her nephew. The Earl was severely neat as ever. He was not given to extravagance in dress, and Elizabeth had to concede that his tall figure needed no adornment. His cravat was simply tied *en cascade* while his nephew, mistakenly in her opinion, had adopted the Byronic fashion. Taken in conjunction with a coat of just too bright a blue, cut with exaggeratedly wide lapels, it made him look shorter than his actual inches. Beside his uncle he presented the appearance of a cheerful untidy schoolboy. Nevertheless the open admiration on his good-natured countenance was very sweet, as he came forward to greet her in his easy-going way.

"By jove, Miss Kirkley, you bloom like the roses themselves. The air of Anderley must suit your constitution. Will you be sorry to leave when the season calls you back to London, or are you pining for the delights of town? Mama is making any number of plans for your entertainment, and I shall certainly claim proprietary rights as your escort. What a score for me to be first in the field with one who is clearly destined to become the rage!"

These practised and exaggerated gallantries were no more than the common currency of polite small talk, but they were fresh to Elizabeth's ears and she found them exhilarating. She blushed, laughed and disclaimed, and allowed the gentleman to give her his arm in to dinner, Lady Hester indulgently renouncing her own claim and declaring that the children would do very much better to amuse each other. In this they succeeded to admiration, Timothy keeping his partner in a bubble of laughter with a lively account of his journey north. He had the happy knack of making perfectly commonplace incidents appear amusing, and if, in the telling, truth was twisted out of all recognition, why—it was all perfectly harmless; and the girl was such a stimulating audience, seeming to hang upon his words, that Timothy quite excelled himself. Lady Hester watched contentedly. She had grown sincerely fond of Elizabeth, and Timothy was really a dear boy, perfectly good-natured and generous to a fault. Naturally he was a little bored and impatient with Richard's solemn notions of responsibility. He was young and gay. Time enough to grow serious when he was married and settled. She beamed approvingly upon the young people, and her brother, deep in discussion with Miss Trenchard on the possibilities of the railways as future carriers of passengers, also spared them an occasional measuring glance.

If Timothy secretly thought that the projected morning parties sounded insipid to a degree, he put a good face on the matter, promptly soliciting Elizabeth's hand for the first quadrille. With equal good nature he faced the prospect of the mild excitements of whist, as played by the three ladies—the tyro Elizabeth, the fiercely acquisitive Miss Trenchard, and the absent-minded Lady Hester. Evenings, he decided, swallowing a yawn, were the one disadvantage of a stay at Anderley. There was no denying it—they were damnably dull. A light flirtation might have enlivened the present game, but Elizabeth, who had unfortunately cut Miss Trenchard as her partner, was much too busy trying to remember what she had been taught about leads and discards to respond to his tentative openings. By the time that Lady Hester had twice in one hand enquired what were trumps, he could only be thankful for the early arrival of the tea tray. Tomorrow, he decided, he would suggest teaching Miss Kirkley to play billiards. That would at least provide better scope for gentle dalliance.

Chapter Nine

And now time passed swiftly for Elizabeth. Mr Elsford's companionship seemed to supply just what had previously been lacking—a contemporary to share her pursuits and interests. They were never at a loss for occupation or food for argument. What with looking over the hound puppies who would join the Anderley pack when cubbing began, trying out the horses, both riding and driving, and exploring parts of the countryside hitherto forbidden to Elizabeth because they lay outside the boundaries of the estate, her leisure hours were full of varied interest.

Thanks to Miss Clara, she was quite unusually knowledgeable about crops and stock, and since she had the instinctive feminine cunning to play intelligent pupil to Mr Elsford's tutorship, that young man was moved to inform his uncle that never would he have believed that a mere female could have so sound an instinct for the management of land. The Earl, who had been privileged to meet Miss Clara and had a pretty shrewd idea of the source of Elizabeth's surprising ability, received the confidence without undue emotion, merely raising a sardonic eyebrow.

Master Timothy's idle plans for a pleasant flirtation with Miss Kirkley had not met with the easy success that he had anticipated. His most subtle compliments only served to amuse her, and she showed not a trace of that maidenly confusion that it would have been his pleasure to allay. As for his attempts to guide her hands in the proper manipulation of billiard cue or driving reins, she simply moved away from him. Her cool detachment had done her no disservice in the young man's eyes. Between the mild boredom of country society, the growing attraction of an increasingly vivid and alluring Elizabeth, and her present air of unattainability, Mr Elsford was almost inclined to believe that this time his affections were seriously engaged.

Only once was their pleasant comradeship disturbed, and that was when Elizabeth suggested that they might visit Lucy Bassett. They had been returning from a long afternoon's ride by a green track that passed quite close to the cottage. Elizabeth was warm and thirsty. A cool drink would be pleasant. Also, thanks to the inroads that Mr Elsford had made upon her time, it was close upon two weeks since she had ridden this way. She spoke to him of Lucy, reminding him that, though he had probably never set eyes upon her, yet she had been, at one time, in his mother's service and would no doubt value a visit from him. She wondered a little whether she ought to mention the existence of Mally, but since it was difficult to explain in such words as a young lady might use with propriety, decided not to make the attempt.

Even while she hesitated Mr Elsford announced coldly that he had no smallest intention of making such a visit, and indeed wondered very much that Miss Kirkley had chosen to do so. Far from not remembering Lucy Bassett, it seemed that he knew all about her and did not consider her a suitable acquaintance for his companion. His censorious attitude annoyed Elizabeth. *He* had no right to appoint himself an arbiter of *her* conduct, and it was with mischievous satisfaction that she told him that the Earl himself had introduced her to Lucy.

That certainly gave Mr Elsford pause, but only briefly. What might be perfectly proper in a man of his uncle's years and notorious carelessness of public opinion was not necessarily allowable to an innocent young lady. And while no word of criticism should pass his lips, he could not feel that his uncle had acted with due consideration when he allowed the girl to come back to Anderley. Progressive ideas and Christian charity were all very well, but the girl and her child had been well provided for and she should have been content to hide herself away at a decent distance.

Remembering the savage isolation of the cottage and Lucy's desperate loneliness, Elizabeth was fiercely indignant. For the first time in their acquaintance she suddenly recognised in Mr Elsford's sullen expression a strong resemblance to his haughty Mama. Battle between them was fairly joined, and both participants hotly maintained their respective principles. It was the kind of squabble that is wholly unprofitable. Timothy, hedged about by prejudice, was quite incapable of moderating his attitude, while Elizabeth was arguing from one special case which had touched her sympathies. Long before she had exhausted her passionate defence, Timothy had retreated behind a barrier of silence—sulky or dignified according to one's point of view. The ride ended in an atmosphere of mutual displeasure, and for the rest of the evening they were meticulously polite to one another.

It was unfortunate that the next day was the one appointed for the first party. In the nervousness natural to the occasion, Elizabeth would have been very glad of friendly support. A small private joke, a word of praise for her appearance, would have helped to pluck up her courage. But Timothy was still on his high ropes. He had grown accustomed to Elizabeth's unquestioning acquiescence in all matters of social conduct and could not lightly forgive her defection. Virtuously he assured himself that his duties as host left him no time for paying her any special attention. He was her partner in the first quadrille, in which she performed her part with care and dignity, though her serious expression would not have satisfied M. d'Aubiac.

Partners came and went, some once-met, some total strangers, until her mind was a whirl of half-caught and half-remembered names and faces, and she fulfilled her part in the dancing more and more mechanically. Conversation was the worst bugbear. By the end of the first hour she was beginning to wonder if an uncommonly dry season had ever been so thoroughly discussed before. By the middle of the second she was thankful for even this outworn topic. All her partners seemed to expect her to be perfectly *au fait* with all the latest stories of the 'ton', and, of course, she had nothing to contribute. When, in desperation, she spoke of the beauty of the surrounding countryside, they could only say that it was sad hunting country, though the moors certainly afforded some good sport in the season. Her timid interest in the country folk and their means of livelihood occasioned only stares of blank stupefaction.

The morning to which she had looked forward with eager interest was rapidly developing into a kind of mechanical nightmare in which one moved and spoke with a sense of complete unreality, yet was all the time aware of critical watching eyes. Elizabeth could not know that she was the subject of much interested speculation. No one knew the exact truth of her parentage, or the size of her fortune, yet here she was, apparently very much at home, and going about everywhere with that extremely eligible bachelor, Timothy Elsford, for whom at least half of the young ladies present entertained secret ambitions.

That was not counting Primrose Bentley, for this was the first time that she had swum into Mr Elsford's ken. Indeed Lady Hester had hesitated long over the vexed problem of issuing an invitation to that young lady. Undoubtedly she was well connected on the maternal side, but no one could deny that her grandfather had been in trade. It was only because she was staying with her Aunt Considine, unencumbered by her plebian and ridiculously wealthy papa, that the scales had tipped in her favour. After all, an invitation to this sort of party was of no particular significance, and in no way committed one for the future. So Miss Bentley's young heart was gladdened by the coveted invitation, and here she was, looking absurdly like her name flower with her pale golden hair and her soft green gown, her wide gaze lifted in awed admiration to her resplendent partner. And Mr Elsford, for his part, handed her to her place in the set as though she were made of fragile spun glass.

Elizabeth's partner had no such delicate notions. She liked Mr Maxton, amiable and fat as he was, but there was no denying that his dancing was compounded largely of energy and goodwill. It was fortunate that they had reached the bottom of the set before he managed to step on the side of her sandal and snap the cord fastening, for she was thus able to withdraw to effect the necessary repairs without breaking up the whole dance.

Lady Hester had appointed a small saloon behind the ballroom for the convenience of the ladies, and here her own maid, Janet, and young Edith were in eager attendance, thoroughly enjoying the novelty of a change in the day's routine. The sandal string was beyond repair, and Edith went scampering upstairs to bring down fresh ones, only to check abruptly as the majestic figure of the housekeeper swam into view. Mrs Jessup eyed her forbiddingly, but for once offered no reproof. That stern eye was sufficient. Edith continued on her errand in more subdued style, though once around the corner she wrinkled her snub little nose in a derisive grimace.

Elizabeth, who was in no hurry to return to the ballroom, made no complaint over the girl's tardy return, and even asked her to fix a curl which had descended from its proper place in the carefully careless knot on top of her head. Then, with a tiny sigh, she turned away from the mirror, thanked the maids for their help and went slowly back along the corridor. She paused for a moment at the door, listening to the sounds of music and merriment within. There could be no more than two or three remaining dances to be endured. She had at least acquitted herself fairly creditably on the dance floor. And if she had found the morning a sad disappointment it was probably quite her own fault for expecting too much. With an almost defiant little lift of her head she went back into the ballroom.

From the first turn of the great staircase the Earl had watched her movements with close attention. Something was clearly amiss. What should have been a morning of unclouded pleasure had evidently become an ordeal to be endured. He had not failed to notice the obvious gathering of her courage to face the battery of inquisitive eyes. Where Miss Kirkley was concerned, he decided with cynical detachment, he was becoming quite unnaturally perceptive.

His intention had been to take refuge in the library until the festivities should be safely over. Now he turned back to his own apartments. Never, even in his military days, when sudden alarms had caused him to don uniform and accoutrements in furious haste, had he dressed with more celerity. The bell that summoned his man had scarcely ceased to quiver before he had discarded his dusty riding clothes and was splashing water over his head and shoulders. To terse, unbelievable commands the valet was helping him into the fawn pantaloons, the olive green cutaway coat of formal day wear, shocked into unwonted silence by the lightning speed with which his master was adjusting his neckcloth, even while admitting that the result was, as ever, impeccable.

"You may relax, Wilson," came the cool sardonic voice, as the Earl crossed to the door in a couple of swift strides. "I believe I have not yet taken leave of my senses."

The door closed behind him, and the bewildered valet was left to survey a welter of untidily discarded clothing such as he had never beheld in all the years of his service with his lordship. Sorrowfully he lifted the ill-treated riding coat, only to reveal a far more shocking sight, a sight which caused him to entertain grave doubts as to the truth of his lordship's parting remarks. In his insensate, his *criminal* haste, the Earl had actually removed his boots with a jack!

Chapter Ten

Only the waltz cotillon now, reckoned Elizabeth thankfully, going down the set with a cheerful youth who had just bidden a final farewell to Oxford and was quite wild with delight at returning to the freedom of his ancestral acres. She could not remember who he was, but found him pleasantly conversable and was quite sorry when her next partner came up to claim the last dance. As luck would have it they made up a set with Mr Elsford and Miss Bentley, dancing together for the third time. Mr Elsford at least ought to know better, thought Elizabeth soberly. He could have little thought for the child, exposing her to the criticism of all the neighbourhood. She directed upon him a glance of serious reproof which he entirely misunderstood, setting it down to the fact that he had not asked her for a second dance. He smiled at her beguilingly, his resentment all forgotten. She was well enough, Miss Kirkley, a good sort of girl, as he had stoutly maintained to his Mama, even if a trifle revolutionary in some of her notions, but beside the adorable Miss Bentley with her faintly flushed cheeks and her huge worshipping eyes, she paled into insignificance, he decided, as he swept his bows to both ladies and swung into the first figure.

So that was it, thought the Earl, coming quietly into the ballroom through one of the tall windows that stood open to the terrace. Master Timothy playing off his tricks. Yet another pretty face. He shrugged and wondered idly who the chit might be, and whether his nephew would always flit lightly from flower to flower. His wife would probably have to accustom herself to his philanderings, but no doubt there were any number of girls who would not mind, and would only too gladly pick up the handkerchief if Timothy chose to drop it. He was beginning to doubt, however, if Miss Kirkley was of their number.

He stood quietly watching the dancers, as yet unnoticed save by his sister. Then, as the music died and the flood of talk and laughter began to swell again, moved across to the little dais where the musicians were established and spoke for a moment with M. d'Aubiac. The old man's face lit up with pleasure but he spread his hands wide in a deprecating gesture and his eyes sought Lady Hester's with a hint of rueful appeal. The Earl smiled, patted him lightly on the shoulder, and crossed to where his sister was standing wondering what in the world he was about. By this time all the eyes in the room were upon him, one or two of the older guests looking startled, even mildly affronted by this unheralded arrival of their absentee host, the younger ones obviously delighted, for to most of them he was little more than a legend, so rarely did he put in an appearance at a purely social function. The glamour of his military career still hung about him, and though he was reputed to hold very unorthodox views on the established social hierarchy, yet his wealth, his rank, and most of all his unattainability—for it must be supposed that at five and thirty he was not now likely to marry—all conspired to make him quite deliciously exciting.

"How exactly like Richard," thought the indignant Lady Hester, "to behave in such a shockingly casual fashion." She had apologised so carefully on his behalf, explaining that urgent estate business had made it quite impossible for him to be present this morning as he had so much wished to be. And there he was, quite unrepentant, charming them all into delighted acceptance of his tardy arrival, speaking of his great disappointment at being obliged to miss the party, when she knew very well that he had ridden out especially early on purpose to avoid it, and craving their indulgence for just one more dance. A gentle ripple of delighted assent ran round the room, and several young ladies peeped hopefully under their lashes at the Earl. But he was not quite done.

"Fortunately there is no one here to carry tales of our simple country festivities to the arbiters of London society, so this one dance is to be my favourite—a waltz."

There was an outburst of laughter, and several people turned smilingly to Lady Hester. She shook her head and threw up her hands in mock despair, for in spite of repeated pleas from the eager dancers, she had steadfastly refused to permit them this indulgence. They were all, she had insisted, by far too young.

The Earl held up his hand once more and the amused asides were stilled. "And since I can see several hopeful gentlemen preparing to anticipate me in asking my ward to dance, let me say at once that I intend to stand on the rights of a guardian and claim that honour for myself."

Such was the power of personal magnetism that several gentlemen who had not had the least intention of asking Miss Kirkley to dance groaned aloud, while the boy from Oxford who had indeed formed the intention shook a playful fist at one whom he admired wholeheartedly, having found him to be a first-rate fellow, a capital shot, and one who was always willing to give an aspiring youngster a few hints without being patronising. Elizabeth blushed delightfully and dropped her guardian a shy little curtsy as he crossed the floor to her side. The young ladies consoled themselves with easier, if less exciting, partners, and the one or two older people present assured each other that it had been very prettily done. Whatever his queer philosophies, the Earl's manners, they agreed, were above reproach. Since he could only dance with one young lady, then certainly that one should be his ward, for how could he possibly single out any one of his guests for such particular attention without appearing to slight the rest?

Only Lady Hester, noting the glowing look on Elizabeth's face, was a little doubtful. It was to be hoped that Richard would be careful. When he chose to exert that wicked charm of his he could woo the heart out of a girl's breast, and he himself, case-hardened bachelor that he was, had none to lose. She had trusted that Elizabeth, resentful of his authority and pleasantly preoccupied with Timothy, would be immune. She turned her attention to her nephew and uttered a tiny scandalised moan. It was really too bad of him. He was actually dancing the waltz with Miss Bentley. The Earl's vagaries might be forgiven him—and if he must choose to arrive at the last moment at his own party he had at least carried it off beautifully. She had no hope at all that Timothy's outrageous behaviour would meet with a similar tolerance. She blamed herself for having invited Miss Bentley, but how could she have guessed that the girl would turn out to be such a honey pot? Plainly she had bewitched Timothy, driving all sense of decency from his head, and any hope of his now developing a genuine tendre for Elizabeth must be abandoned.

Once again that delicious sense of floating blissfully on a strong tide, held securely from all harm. Elizabeth surrendered wholeheartedly to the spell of the music and a perfect partner. The Earl held her firmly but quite lightly, yet she was instantly responsive to each movement of his. It was a delightful presentation of the art of the waltz, save that neither obeyed the code which prescribed airy conversation as its accompaniment. They danced in complete silence. Only when the music ended and the Earl was bowing over her hand, very much in the grand manner, did he murmur wickedly so that only she could hear, "If my ward were only so submissive and biddable as my dancing partner, what a very contented guardian I should be." Elizabeth was snatched out of her dreamy languor to laugh and take the arm that he offered to lead her out on to the terrace.

The morning was so warm that Lady Hester had decided no harm could come of permitting the young people to stroll out of doors for a while, and tables had been set under the great cedar tree where Harrison and his minions were dispensing champagne cup and iced lemonade to the thirsty dancers. The Earl procured a glass of lemonade for Elizabeth but took no refreshment himself, declaring that one all-too-short waltz had not made him thirsty. He stood a little way apart as she sipped the cool drink, surveying his partner with that same steady measuring look that she had thought so detestable in the early days of their acquaintance. Somehow this morning she found herself accepting it quite calmly, her eyelids no longer drooping in embarrassment but lifted to return his gaze with one of amused enquiry. This evidently pleased him, for he gave her his infrequent lazy smile and said gently, "You are quite right to wear blue, Miss Kirkley. The rose and the white and the yellow—yes—they become you well enough, but it is the blue that reflects the glow in your eyes."

The eyes in question widened at this very gallant speech, and the soft lips parted in surprise, but the Earl went on quite calmly, almost impersonally, "The gown is in excellent taste, unusual, modest and becoming. I particularly like the restrained elegance of the trimming," and he indicated the delicate scatter of crystals that appeared to have fallen haphazard across tight-fitting bodice and sweeping skirt. "Very refreshing after the profusion of flounces, ruffles and braiding which are become so commonplace. You are in the way of becoming a fashion setter, my child. I make you my compliments." And he sketched her a tiny bow.

"It was a very *expensive* gown, my lord," she said demurely, hands meekly folded together, eyes modestly downcast. And then, with a mischievous upward gleam, "But since it has earned your lordship's approval, I must think the money well-spent."

"I am flattered of course. But it is really quite shocking in you to intrude such mercenary considerations upon my poetic vision of dew-drenched bluebells under spring sunshine," he murmured soulfully, though a deep indentation at the corner of his mouth belied the solemn words.

"Is that how gentlemen of fashion talk? I must say it sounds remarkably foolish to me. But it is kind of you to give me the experience of hearing it, my lord," said Elizabeth cheerfully.

He laughed. "You are fast growing into an impudent brat," he told her, "and that is what any man of sense would certainly say. But for your information, no, I do not think you will find many fashionable gentlemen indulging in quite such ridiculous flights. Perhaps the odd aesthete, seeking to make himself appear something out of the common run. Nevertheless," he teased her, "I trust you will concede that the bluebell notion was quite well thought out. On the spur of the moment, too, since I could not know what colour you would choose to wear." And he grinned at her like a schoolboy enjoying a successful prank.

Elizabeth simply could not resist. "Alas! It seems that some gentlemen prefer primroses to bluebells, my lord," she said mournfully, but with lips that quivered into irrepressible laughter.

He was swift to catch the reference. "Is that indeed her name?" he demanded, and at Elizabeth's nod went on, "I have always been against the practice of bestowing fanciful names on helpless infants. We had a poor devil of a subaltern in the Regiment whose romantic Mama had cursed him with the name of Galahad. You may imagine how we roasted him! I daresay his experiences on the battlefield seemed comparatively pleasant after the sufferings he had endured from his friends. But in this case the child's parents seem to have been positively prophetic. She really does look like a primrose."

Since this remark seemed to be well received, Elizabeth venturing the opinion that Miss Bentley was quite the loveliest girl she had ever seen, he risked a further question. "Timothy seems to be quite *épris*," he suggested.

Elizabeth looked faintly troubled. "Yes, indeed. And I am sure one cannot wonder at it. But I fear he is doing her no service in making her quite so conspicuous. *She* is probably too young to have thought of appearances, but he—" She broke off.

"How many times has he danced with her?" asked the Earl.

"Three or four," admitted Elizabeth, knowing perfectly well that it was four. "And you perceive that he has not left her side since the waltz ended. But I expect he feels that your presence relieves him of any further responsibilities as host," she added excusingly.

"Stupid young idiot," said the Earl dispassionately. "But it would be pointless for me to interfere at this stage. That would only serve to focus attention on a regrettable situation. Who *is* the child, by the way?"

But though Elizabeth was able to tell him her name he could not immediately place her, and dismissed the matter from his thoughts. His nephew's social career had been frequently marred by similar solecisms, and this one did not seem to be of any particular importance. He was more concerned to assure himself that Mr Elsford's defection was not distressing his ward. It would seem that the attachment between them had not gone near so deep as he had believed. Nevertheless it was ridiculous for him to feel so absurdly lighthearted about it. He had promised Charles to do his best to arrange a suitable match for his daughter, and failing Timothy the task was all to do again. Nor could he readily think of a suitable candidate. His requirements in a possible husband for his ward were growing more and more particular. Even Timothy he had always regarded as rather too much of a lightweight—gay and amiable enough when all went smoothly but unpredictable in a crisis, his chief recommendation being that he could offer his wife a position of the first consequence. And the Earl was gradually coming to believe that his ward cared as little for consequence as he did himself. Certainly his own exalted rank had never seemed to overawe her in the least. His mouth twitched in an involuntary grin, remembering some of the choicer epithets that she had hurled at him on the day when she had stumbled on the scene of the deer slaughter.

Elizabeth had been standing quietly sipping her lemonade, content in what seemed to her a companionable silence. She would have liked to know what thought had made him smile so suddenly, but did not like to intrude upon his reverie. Now, however, she felt that she really must draw his attention to a figure which seemed oddly out of place among the elegant company assembled on the lawns. The groom, Hanson, who had been away for several weeks on some errand for his master, was standing on the edge of the terrace looking about him anxiously. Even as Elizabeth touched the Earl's sleeve to draw his attention to the man, Hanson caught sight of the two of them in the deep shadow of the cedar, and began to weave his way through the gay, gossiping throng towards them.

"This means trouble, if I mistake not," said the Earl regretfully. "Miss Kirkley, I must beg you to excuse me. Much as it grieves me to cut short this delightful interlude, I must see what John wants. He would not be seeking me out in this mêlée if it were not urgent. Shall I take you back to my sister?"

"No, indeed, my lord. You will not be wanting to waste time if John's errand is so important. I will go—why, no! This gentleman will escort me back to the house." and she smiled at the boy from Oxford who had been hovering hopefully in the vicinity on the chance of a few more words with this charming and sensible female.

The Earl swung round to see whom she meant. That one errant eyebrow shot up, and he gave a soft crack of laughter. Once again he favoured his ward with a slight teasing bow. "May I congratulate you once more on your good taste, Miss Kirkley? I shall be well content to leave you with Ecclesfield." He lingered only for a word with Elizabeth's chosen escort, then strolled off to meet John. The young man, grinning responsively to his host's teasing quip, came at once to Elizabeth's side.

She was quite scarlet with confusion and scarcely knew how to phrase her apologies to the young Marquis for not having remembered who he was. He only chuckled, and said with good-humoured scorn, "Oh! That fusty old stuff! Time enough to stand upon my rank when I've done something to show I'm fit to hold it. I was hoping to have the chance of another word with you. Do you think Anderley would bring you over to my place some time? The thing is, I've got the sweetest pure-bred mare you ever saw, but my sister says she's a mite too spirited for a lady. I'd value your opinion, for Anderley says you're a capital horsewoman."

He was full of eager talk of his horses, and of a litter of hound puppies whose dam had unfortunately died and who were being reared by his favourite pointer bitch, and since this was just the kind of familiar countrified talk that Elizabeth could understand and enjoy, the pair of them were soon so engrossed that they were quite unaware of the covert interest with which most of the guests, especially the feminine ones, were watching their sauntering progress towards the house. One or two indignant damsels were wondering what was the peculiar charm about the attractive but by no means dazzling Miss Kirkley which had held the Earl of Anderley chained to her side for a good twenty minutes to the exclusion of all other females, and which, apparently, operated equally powerfully upon the shy and hitherto unapproachable Marquis. They could only conclude that her fortune must be enormous. Indeed, the only pair who were entirely unaware of Miss Kirkley's incredible triumph were Mr Elsford and Miss Bentley, who were entirely absorbed in each other.

Since the Marquis stayed close to Elizabeth's side during the serving of the cold collation, himself attending to all her wants, and then persuaded her to walk with him to the stables so that she might see the team of matched chestnuts that he had elected to drive that day, it was quite a question as to whether she or Miss Bentley provided the homeward-going guests with the most food for talk and speculation.

Chapter Eleven

"You're sure it was the smallpox?"

"Well, Sir, I've no medical knowledge, but as sure as a man may be who's seen as much as you and me have of that foul sickness."

"He never regained his senses? Could you not tell who he was, or where he came from?"

Hanson shook his head. "He was anear gone when we picked him up. All I know for sure is that he was a pedlar, and on the road 'twixt Anderley and Coldstone, though whether coming or going there was no telling, save that nobody in Coldstone seemed to have seen him passing through. There was the usual women's gear in his pack, needles and ribbons and such, but there were toys as well—wooden puppets and monkeys to set dancing on strings. If he's passed through the village selling his wares, God knows what might come of it. I reckoned I'd best bring the news right away, Sir, and bring it myself."

The Earl nodded agreement. "To be sending messages of such import might well start a panic. I'll cause enquiries to be made discreetly as to whether any such person has been seen in the neighbourhood. Now—tell me—how does Garrett go on at Coldstone?"

John shook his head. "I'm worried about him, too, Sir," he confessed, shamefaced at having to unload such a burden of troubles on to his master's shoulders. "He was well enough at first, and eager about all the fresh birds and beasts he'd seen. Then he took to wandering up to the quarry. I was fearful he might be thinking to do himself an injury, for he was sullen and broody-like. But he never went near the face. Just hung about and watched the men at work. They're a rough crowd up there, but I will say they were good to him after I'd explained how he came to be the way he was. Shared their bait with him many a time. And the fellow that runs the quarry was in the army himself—Engineer Corps—said he was harmless enough and to let him alone. Times, when he's in a good mood, he'll lend them a hand. And you know his strength, Sir. Why, I've seen him lift rocks with no trouble at all that three men could scarce shift. So you might say he seemed happy enough. And yet somehow I don't like the feel of it. He's gone quiet on me. Never talks about the wild creatures like he used to do, and there's a look in his eye now and now, sort of calculating, that I've not seen before. I can't help thinking he's up to mischief, though what it might be is more than I can guess."

The Earl sighed. "I had hoped that if we got him away from here to some remote spot like Coldstone where he could watch his beloved wild things to his heart's content, he might quieten down. Dr Hartwell is for ever hinting that he should be put under restraint, but the thought of it is horrible. He's gently bred and educated, John, indeed a brilliant scholar I was told. And then a head wound in battle, and his mind is gone beyond repair. No living relatives—or none who would claim and care for him. At least with me he has a measure of freedom. Does he still take pleasure in watching the wild creatures?"

"Oh, aye," nodded John. "There's an old badger's holt up in the woods above the quarry. He's up there night after night watching the varmints. Then he'll sleep the morning away, like as not. I've kept my eye on him as best I could, but short of locking him in, which you particularly forbade, there's no watching him all the time. He can slip away as soft as a shadow for all his size."

"Poor John! I ask too much of you, I know. Shall I send your brother and young Ned over to Coldstone in your place? I'd be very willing to keep you with me for, strangely enough, I've missed you. It seems one can grow so accustomed to being bullied and over-ruled at every hand's turn that one positively feels the lack of it."

John reddened a little at the affectionate note in the Earl's voice, and grinned at the teasing. "This is no time for your funning, Sir," he said severely. "Of course I'm going back to Coldstone. Truth to tell I didn't above half like leaving him, but he was sound asleep, having been out most of the night, and I asked the lads at the quarry to look out for him. I'll be off back now. But, Sir, if there should be sickness and trouble here, you'd let me come back then, wouldn't you?"

"But of course!" said the Earl solemnly. "I should send for you at once. I am well aware that I could not possibly manage for myself, and naturally no consideration for your health and safety would prevent me from summoning you to my assistance."

"And it had better not," retorted his retainer grimly. "I'm not saying anything against poor Mr Garrett—indeed I'm heart sorry for him, but if there's bad sickness here in the village, then my place is here with you, and that's where I'm going to be, orders or no orders."

"As you say, you insubordinate old villain," submitted the Earl meekly. "But don't I wish I had you back in the army again! Only time in my life that you ever took notice of my orders! See that you get a meal before you start back. And understand that Garrett is *my* responsibility. If he makes trouble, you are not to be blamed. To be keeping watch over a man of unbalanced mind who is quite unpredictable in his moods and movements is a heavy task. Indeed only a fool like John Hanson would be willing to undertake it. No, don't argue," as John opened his mouth to protest, "I know very well it is asking too much of you. But I do ask it, for I can think of no other man who would do it one half so well. Only, if he should give you the slip, you're not to go fretting yourself to flinders, for it will not be your fault. Now, be off with you. And remember—a good meal and a fresh nag," and with a valedictory slap on the tall groom's shoulder he went off to the library to consider what precautions would need to be taken in the event of an outbreak of smallpox.

Country people were notoriously suspicious of new-fangled notions and slow to adopt them, so few, if any, of the villagers would have been vaccinated, but he could probably reckon that more than half of the adult population would already have had the disease. They were safe enough. The worst danger was to the children, and little use trying to persuade them to accept vaccination now. All he could do was decide on a suitable building to which sufferers could be carried—always supposing that their relatives would consent—and ensure that a sufficient supply of palliasses and blankets and all the other impedimenta of a fever hospital should be available in case of need. He started to make lists, with a passing thought that John's advice would have been invaluable, for John, less fortunate than his master, had spent one or two spells in army hospitals. Mentally he reviewed the other members of his vast household. Only his ward gave him cause for anxiety. Had she been vaccinated? Dare he make direct enquiry? He shook his head. That quick mind of hers would jump to the obvious conclusion at the least hint. He must not put the burden of fear upon those young shoulders, but guard her as best he could from any risk of infection. The other inmates of Anderley had meekly accepted vaccination upon entering his employment. It was reckoned to be just part of the master's eccentricity, and Lady Hester herself had set the example. Despite that hideous obstacle of compulsory vaccination, there was still considerable competition for places at Anderley. Should the need arise, there would be no lack of nursing orderlies either. And Hester could be trusted to deal admirably with the domestic side of the business. A first-rate Quartermaster General was lost when Hester was born a woman, he reflected.

He pushed the lists aside, then, on second thoughts, pressed the spring that opened a secret compartment in the desk and laid them away in greater safety. He would drive down to the village and try if indirect enquiry would elicit any information about the dead pedlar.

The evidence was inconclusive, though on the whole favourable. None of the children were playing with such toys as John had described, and when he ventured on oblique enquiry, suggesting casually that if a pedlar should chance to come to the village the maids at Anderley would doubtless be glad of the opportunity to buy a few fripperies, he met only a shake of the head and a voluble outpouring of regret that no such interesting visitor had been seen for an age. But since it then transpired that the speaker had recently been away from home at her sister's lying-in, he could not take solid comfort from this, and dare not repeat the enquiry, since assuredly the good ladies would subsequently compare notes on what he had said, and it would certainly puzzle them to know what the Earl had been wanting so urgently with a pedlar man.

He said all that was proper about the interesting family event, thankful that, since the sister did not reside upon the Anderley estate, he would neither be asked to stand sponsor nor hear that the infant was to be endowed with his Christian name, and turned towards home, his mind a little relieved of its burden of anxiety. Perhaps the pedlar had, after all, been heading *towards* Anderley when his illness struck him down. Thankfully he turned his thoughts to less solemn matters.

The possibility of a match between his ward and his nephew appeared to be receding. That was wasteful but not tragic. The girl had the makings of a good châtelaine and would have lent ballast to young Timothy, who stood sorely in need of it. Anderley could use a girl of that calibre, whereas his nephew's latest *inamorata* appeared to be purely ornamental. *That* she certainly was, but whether there was either intelligence or character behind the lovely face was yet to be seen. She had not, apparently, attracted young Ecclesfield. And Ecclesfield was sound as a roast and could pick out a well-bred 'un with the best; as witness his immediate liking for Elizabeth. For some time now the Earl had been permitting himself in private the luxury of calling his ward by her beautiful given name. He could not help feeling a glow of satisfaction, even of pride, that Ecclesfield should have taken so strong a fancy to her. It was a just tribute to her quality. A pity that the lad was not ten years older, or—it was out in the open at last—that he himself was not ten years younger. He frowned, remembering some careless words that his sister Maria had once spoken about the strong possibility of his marrying in his dotage. Well—he was not in his dotage yet. Some would say that thirty-five was the prime of life. But it was far too old to wed with twenty-three, especially a twenty-three so young and inexperienced as Elizabeth Kirkley's, even if his overbearing ways had not caused the girl to take him in dislike at their very first meeting. Of late, it was true, there had been signs of softening in her attitude, and when they had danced together the Earl would have been prepared to vow that she liked him very well. But with the whimsical folly of a sensible man already far deeper in love than he knew, he decided that, as they could scarcely spend the rest of their lives dancing together, he had best put temptation aside. But neither would he squander valuable time in searching the ranks of his acquaintance for a match for Elizabeth. There was no call for undue haste. It would be another six months before she could be presented. Time enough then, he decided light-heartedly, to set about the business in earnest.

He was whistling cheerfully as he re-entered his house, affronting the staid Harrison, who considered such behaviour quite unsuited to the consequence of an Earl, and his mellow mood was not even dissipated by the knowledge that he had made little progress in his enquiries, nor by Hester's mournful recital of the catalogue of Timothy's sins. Timothy, it appeared, had crowned a morning of reckless indiscretion by insisting that he must escort Miss Bentley back to her Aunt's house. Who knew, he said stoutly, what dangers she might not meet between Anderley and Abbey House? Lady Hester, enquiring bitterly if there was any latent madness in the Elsford family, found her brother quite undisturbed. If Timothy must run mad, he said lazily, better here than in Town. And if he was so besotted about his Primrose, he had best marry her and be done with it.

Such flippancy did nothing to soothe his sister. "Primrose!" she snorted. "A modest flower, or so the poets would have us believe. This one should have been called Peony—flaunting herself abroad like a travelling raree show, with a gentleman escort needed for a journey of three miles in broad daylight!" And was sadly discomposed when her brother only laughed, and quite refused to speak seriously to his nephew about his rash and foolish behaviour.

Chapter Twelve

Elizabeth supposed that one was bound to find life a little flat and depressing after the excitement of the party, but it was distinctly lowering to find that the mood was so long-lived. It was only to be expected that she should miss her monopoly of Timothy's cheerful company, but she had rather shyly hoped that, after the distinguishing attention that her guardian had bestowed upon her at the party, she might have been vouchsafed a little more of *his* society. She still regarded him with some doubt and puzzlement, but he was interesting, even exciting, and when he wished he could be kind. There was no denying that her initial resentment was fading fast in face of his charm.

But instead of an improvement in their relations there came a slight setback when the Earl issued orders that she was not to ride into the village. He gave no reason for this limitation of her freedom, and since he had very unfairly obtained her promise of obedience by asking first if she would be willing to oblige him in a small matter, she was unable to show her opinion of such arbitrary treatment by open defiance.

She still spent a good deal of her time with Mr Elsford, but it was quite amazing how often they chanced to meet Miss Bentley whenever they went abroad, whether riding with a groom in attendance or walking with one of her several Considine cousins. Elizabeth was inclined to like Miss Bentley, who seemed to be a sweet-natured girl of a gentle and confiding disposition, but a three-cornered riding party was certainly an awkward one. Since Miss Bentley, though well taught, was a timid horsewoman, it generally resolved itself into two sections, one pair riding sedately along the smoother paths while the third member, watched at first anxiously and then in growing admiration by Miss Bentley's groom, skirmished gaily around them, trying out one or other of her guardian's horses over fences and hedges that would have daunted most females. As for the Considine girls, they were a spiritless set, much overborne by their dragon of a mother, and concerned only to play propriety to their pretty cousin. Indeed the only satisfactory and intelligent company to be found on these excursions was that supplied by the horses, thought Elizabeth with a rueful chuckle.

Indoors, Lady Hester seemed unusually preoccupied with domestic matters. The whole household was kept in a bustle over a monumental assembling and checking of stores from blankets to pudding basins. Elizabeth, surveying the operation with puzzled respect, had never dreamed that such very humdrum affairs formed part of the duties of the mistress of a great household. Miss Trenchard's orderly mind rejoiced in the proceedings, and she was promptly enrolled as Lady Hester's lieutenant, busying herself with detailed lists and careful notes of deficiencies to be made good.

When the pair of them did occasionally emerge from this orgy of domesticism, it was to bemoan the folly of Mr Elsford in making such a cake of himself in his pursuit of Miss Bentley, which was the talk of the neighbourhood, or to deplore the absence of the Earl just when he was most needed. What a gentleman could have to contribute to the study of blankets and basins was beyond Elizabeth's imagining, but when she put the question into words her remark created an oddly embarrassed little silence. The two ladies looked at each other guiltily, and Lady Hester hastily murmured something about her brother's army experience having made him more knowledgeable about matters of organisation than most country gentlemen.

The Earl himself was rarely at home. Once Elizabeth met him in the hall as he returned from some protracted expedition. It was probably only a trick of the light, but he looked harassed and weary so that she forgot for the moment that she was at outs with him and would have stopped to ask if aught was amiss, but he brushed past her with no more than a smile and a courteous greeting and disappeared into the library.

It was not long before the prevailing air of unease affected her spirits. She grew increasingly certain that something was being kept from her, and that the something was of a calamitous nature. The conspiracy of silence seemed to exclude only herself and Mr Elsford, for that young gentleman showed no signs of stress other than those natural in a young man of mercurial temperament head over heels in love. Resentment rose within her. If trouble was threatening—vaguely she guessed at some form of rioting such as had been all too common in recent years—then she was not a child to be kept in the dark. She should be allowed to take her share of the burden of anxiety.

It was in this mood that she set off to visit Lucy. She had not ridden up the lonely valley for more than three weeks. Lucy would enjoy hearing about the party and the dresses that the ladies had worn. She might also be able to shed some light on this mysterious cloud that was hanging over Anderley.

She rode at any easy pace, for the day was hot and humid, the sky heavy with the threat of coming storm. Once or twice she looked up at the lowering clouds. Heaven knew the rain was desperately needed, but there was no point in her getting a soaking. She judged that the storm would hold off for two or three hours yet, time enough to be safely home before it broke.

The woods were unusually silent today. There was no current of air to stir the dry leaves, and all the small creatures of the wild seemed to have hidden themselves away. She must be growing foolishly fanciful, she decided, for the stillness struck her as ominous, a brooding waiting for disaster to strike. Impatient with her own nervous fancies, she shook her head as in fierce denial and urged the mare to a gentle trot.

From custom she now rode round to the back of the cottage to see if Lucy and the child were in the garden, but today there was no one there. Someone must be at home though, for there was a pale feather of smoke drifting from the chimney and the door was standing wide open as though the very house were gasping for air. Elizabeth turned the mare loose in the little paddock and walked up the garden path to the front door with a smile for memories thus evoked. There was no immediate answer to her knock. Then she heard the sound of hurrying footsteps coming down the steep stair, and Lucy appeared in the open doorway. But what a changed Lucy! From her haggard face and the bruise-like marks below her eyes she might not have slept for a week. Her hair was unkempt, her body limp and heavy with weariness and her dress spattered and crumpled as though she had lived and slept in it for days.

Recognition of her visitor seemed to galvanise her into fresh life. Her eyes brightened eagerly and she clutched at Elizabeth's hands.

"Oh! Miss Elizabeth! Did his lordship send you? God bless him for the good thought! You will help me to make her better, won't you? She doesn't even know me now. Just lies there muttering and moaning and turning her poor little head from side to side."

As the words poured out she was unconsciously tugging at Elizabeth's hands as though to urge her to come at once to the sick child, and

Elizabeth, her heart full of pity for the poor distraught creature, followed her willingly enough.

Children, she knew, could run a fever from many simple causes; could appear very ill indeed and yet be almost recovered next day. Devoutly she hoped that this might be the case with Mally. But one glance at the little girl dispelled any hope of such a comfortable issue. Here was something far more serious than a simple childish ailment.

"How long has she been like this?" she asked, trying to keep her voice level and not unduly concerned.

Lucy looked at her vaguely. "Three days—four days—I think. She said her head hurt her, and her back. She's been very sick, too. I thought perhaps she'd eaten poison berries, though I've watched her so carefully. She will get better, won't she, Miss Elizabeth?"

Elizabeth stooped over the half-conscious child and smoothed the tangled hair away from the hot forehead, noticing pitifully the cracked lips and the weary restless turning of the little head. Lucy was gazing at her desperately, hopefully, begging for a reassurance that she dare not give.

"If you warmed some water we could bathe her face and limbs," she said gently. "That would cool her a little, and she might sleep. And perhaps a drink—" She hesitated. It was unlikely that a cottage store-room would have lemons. "Perhaps camomile tea, or blackcurrant," she suggested, and as Lucy hurried away, thankful to be given something to do, turned back to the bed and began to straighten the tumbled covers. There was something hard under the sheet. She turned it back to reveal a jointed wooden monkey on strings which could be pulled to make it move in a stiff little dance. Some favourite toy, no doubt, that Lucy had given to the child for comfort. She laid it on the chest of drawers, for Mally would not miss it now, and sat down in the chair beside the bed where Lucy had been keeping her anxious vigil. The child flung out one arm, and Elizabeth took the hot little hand in hers to tuck it back under the bedclothes. As she did so, she noticed the heavy rash of hard spots on the tiny wrist. Her eyes dilated. She had seen spots like that before. This was no case of eating poison berries. Mally had smallpox.

Throughout the hours of the long hot afternoon the two girls tended the child as best they could. It was very hot and stuffy in the tiny bed-chamber under the eaves, for the window was not made to open. In her heavy habit Elizabeth was more than uncomfortable, and wisps of hair clung damply about her flushed face. The sponging with lukewarm water had given the child some relief, and she lay more quietly for a while, but they could not rouse her to drink and had to content themselves with moistening her lips from time to time.

They spoke little, for the sound of their voices seemed to disturb Mally, who would begin to toss and whimper. Once Lucy whispered that his lordship had sent for a physician to come to the child, but since he must come from Slapton it might be late before he arrived. It was indeed past six o'clock when the sound of hoofs sent Lucy hurrying down the stairs, only to come back almost at once with a white, scared face.

"It's not the doctor," she said in an urgent under voice. "It's his lordship. He wants to speak to you. And oh! Miss, I'm afraid he's very angry."

Elizabeth could see no cause for anger, though certainly she had been out for longer than she had first intended. But since she had dutifully left a message to say where she was gone, no one could complain that she had given cause for anxiety. She went softly down the stairs, thinking only of Mally and the need for quiet.

The Earl was standing in the middle of the room, his hands gripping the back of a tall Windsor chair with a force that whitened the knuckles. His lips were so tightly pressed together that they formed a thin hard line, and his eyes were slitted in seething fury. Elizabeth shrank back at the sight of this iron visage. She had never seen him in real anger before, and for a moment it seemed to her that the room was charged with the power radiating from his rigid figure. He seemed poised to annihilate any lesser creature that dared to cross his path. Yet his voice was perfectly under control, though the tone was searing as ice.

"I do not know why you came to this house, Miss Kirkley, or why, having learned that there was dire sickness here, you were so rash and foolish as to remain. But you will return to Anderley at once. Every stitch of your clothing is to be burned immediately, and you will direct your maid to prepare a bath as hot as is endurable. You will then have her scrub every inch of your person until the skin is pink, and also wash your hair. After which you will remain in your own apartments until my physician has seen you."

By the time that he had come to the end of these embarrassingly particular orders, Elizabeth, who had certainly been shaken by the mordant fury of the opening phrases, had quite recovered her composure. To know that the Earl had been moved to such wrath—and indeed to the utterance of such extremely indelicate instructions—by his concern for her safety, could only be a source of deep satisfaction. He would surely not have spoken so if she had been to him just a burden dutifully borne for love of her father. Thus she was able to answer him quite collectedly, though her soft tones were just as determined as his thunderous ones.

"I am sorry to have given cause for anxiety, my lord, and also that I must now incur your grave displeasure by refusing to obey you. I cannot leave that poor girl alone in her anxiety. There is little that anyone can do for the child, but I can at least support and comfort the mother."

The Earl's hands released the chair back. He took two swift strides towards her, caught her by the shoulders and shook her fiercely.

"Crazy little fool!" he bit out. "You will obey me if I have to tie you on the mare and lead her all the way home. That child has smallpox. Do you think I will allow you to risk contracting the disease by nursing her? God alone knows if you are not already infected, but at least we will take no further chances." He made as though to sweep her into his arms and put his threat into execution. Elizabeth managed to fend him off for a moment, catching at his sleeve as she said breathlessly, for the shaking had been no playful make-believe, his lordship having put into it much of his pent-up desperation, "My lord, indeed you are anxious without cause. I shall not take the smallpox from Mally."

His brow cleared. "You have been vaccinated?" he demanded eagerly.

She shook her head. "No. But truly I am quite safe. Dr Jenner would tell you so himself. You are forgetting that I lived in Berkeley and that I had the best of doctors. I had the cowpox as a child, when I would insist on learning how to milk. It seems that if one has had *that* one is quite safe from smallpox. I even helped to nurse one of our maidservants who took the sickness and I came to no harm."

He looked down at her, still holding her between his hands, at the flushed eager face, the tumble of soft brown hair about her shoulders for which his rough handling was responsible, and his grim visage relaxed. Quite unconsciously he breathed a deep sigh of thankfulness. Then a rueful twinkle crept into his eyes.

"And now I suppose it is *my* turn to apologise for jumping too quickly to conclusions," he murmured in comical dismay. "Intemperate language and misuse of brute strength. I can only trust that I have not really hurt you. The rest you must surely forgive, since it was only my concern for your safety that so provoked me." He held out his hands in a gesture of mock supplication as he spoke, and Elizabeth willingly put hers into them, for who could resist the warm, loving look in the grey eyes or the mischievous sideways tilt of the proud head? Though she was pretty sure that her shoulders would bear the marks of those hard fierce fingers for days, and indeed, foolishly, rather hoped that they would, she assured him that she was not in the least hurt but must certainly put her hair to rights. And since a tentative shake of her head completed the ruin, scattering pins all over the floor, the Earl laughed and helped her to pick them up, and the moment of close intimacy was gone.

After she had tidied herself she came back to him and they consulted together soberly as to what was best to be done. Elizabeth stood to it firmly that Lucy knew and trusted her, so no one else, however willing a nurse, could really take her place. To this the Earl eventually yielded. But he insisted that before resuming her post she must first go home, change her habit for a more comfortable dress and eat her dinner. Then she could have herself driven back to the cottage in the light chaise so that she could bring with her various commodities to supplement the limited resources of the cottage. He himself would remain, at least until Bassett came home and possibly until the doctor arrived, so that Lucy should not be left alone. Elizabeth went back to the sickroom to explain these arrangements to Lucy while the Earl saddled up for her.

As he put her up she could not resist teasing him a little. "You will not, after all, tie me to the saddle, my lord? I will do my best, I promise, not to fall off!"

He looked up at her quizzically. "Vindictive little wretch! I thought I had been forgiven! A more generous nature would not advert to past injuries. Be careful, Miss Kirkley, for next time you rebel I shall not waste time on issuing threats!"

She laughed, and rode through the gate that he was holding open for her, tossing back over her shoulder, "Behold me in a positive quake of terror at the thought!" And with a gesture of playful salute from her whip she was on her way.

Chapter Thirteen

All through the grim hours of the night as they fought the losing battle for the child's life, Elizabeth drew strength and courage from a new spring of happiness within herself. She would not yet examine its source. This was not the time nor the place. All her conscious thoughts were devoted to her self-imposed task, but she would not have denied that her genuine sorrow for Lucy was shot through and lightened by the knowledge that the Earl was waiting in the room downstairs, ready to lend aid and support in any crisis. He had ridden back to Anderley after the physician had seen the child, but had returned shortly before midnight, having turned a deaf ear to the indignant protestations of Lady Hester, who had very reasonably pointed out that he would be of no use at all in a sickroom and might indeed be very much in the way.

"I know," he acknowledged. "But I cannot leave Miss Kirkley, who is not even a member of my family, to carry alone a burden that is rightly mine. If, as there seems grave cause to fear, the child should die, I can at least deal with the necessary arrangements, for Miss Kirkley will have her hands full with the mother. The poor creature is near demented with grief and anxiety, and her father, decent fellow though he is, is little comfort to her. He has never reconciled himself to Lucy's situation, and though I am sure he does not positively wish the child dead, he would certainly regard its death as a benevolent dispensation of Providence. So naturally he cannot enter into his daughter's feelings as Miss Kirkley apparently does."

"Really, Richard, you are growing foolish beyond permission," returned his sister, seriously exasperated. "To concern yourself with the well-being of your servants and tenants is doubtless very right and proper. But to carry it to these ridiculous extremes is out of all reason. Do you propose to act nursemaid for every sick child on the estate? You are like to be kept busy! And in this case especially your attentions must present a very odd appearance and cause a great deal of talk. As if it were not enough that the whole neighbourhood is already agog over Timothy's absurd infatuation."

"Which reminds me, where is Timothy?" enquired his uncle, coolly ignoring the rest of the speech.

"He is spending tonight and tomorrow with the Considines," said Lady Hester austerely. "It seems that the young people are all bent on an expedition to Semerwater. Someone seems to have taken a notion that with the level of the lake fallen so low it may be possible to discern traces of the drowned village which is said by legend to lie beneath its waters. Elizabeth was included in the invitation, of course, but she does not seem to have taken to the Considine girls, and I could not think she would find it amusing to watch Timothy dancing attendance on Miss Bentley, so I was really quite thankful that she was out when the scheme was decided on. Though to be sure she would do far better to make one of an innocent pleasure party than to be nursing the child of an abandoned creature like Lucy Bassett."

"Now, Hester! You are permitting your very natural annoyance with me to outweigh your sense of justice. You know very well that you sincerely pitied Lucy, and *I* know equally well the many kindnesses that you have shown her, so let us not dispute further on that head. You shall deplore my mistaken notions of philanthropy as much as you please to our good neighbours."

"That is all very fine talking, Richard, but if only you had taken a wife like a sensible man there would have been no need to involve yourself personally in this sort of philanthropy. Your wife would have dealt with it," retorted his sister, in mild triumph at having scored a point that admitted no argument.

"Now there you are very right, my dear," agreed the Earl as one much struck. "Perhaps I should reconsider the whole question of marriage. But it is, as the Prayer Book reminds us, not to be entered into lightly. So the consideration may wait until tomorrow, and meanwhile I will bid you goodnight. If I am not returned by morning I will send a message to let you know how we go on," and the door closed quietly behind him, leaving his sister, her mouth half open, a prey to mingled amazement and speculation as to his meaning. But after devoting a few moments' thought to the puzzle she decided comfortably that he was only funning. One really could not expect a man of his age to change his mind about the matrimonial state, and his remarks had been much too flippant to be taken seriously.

It was a lonely vigil that the Earl kept in the cottage kitchen, with only the occasional sound of soft footfalls overhead and the chirring of the crickets on the hearth to vary the sound of heavy rain. Bassett had long ago gone to his bed, for a man who rises betimes and works out of doors till close upon dusk needs his sleep. Installed in the high-backed chair, the Earl sat gazing into the glowing embers, and though his reflections appeared to be serious they were not, apparently, sad, for once or twice the hint of a smile touched his mouth.

Some time in the early morning hours Elizabeth came softly downstairs to warm some milk in the hope of persuading Lucy to drink it, for the girl had taken nothing all day. To the query of his lifted brows she shook her head sadly.

"When—if—it is necessary," he said heavily, "Dr Hartwell gave me a draught for Lucy to ensure that she gets some sleep. I fear that it will fall to you, my poor child, to persuade her to swallow it."

Elizabeth looked troubled. "But where *is* she to sleep, my lord? As I judge there are but the two rooms upstairs. If—if anything happens we can scarcely—" She broke off, not wishing to put her fears for Mally into actual words.

"It might be best to carry her back with us to Anderley," said the Earl thoughtfully, "until other arrangements can be made."

The girl nodded agreement. "Yes. I believe you are right. Indeed I would not care to leave her alone if the worst should befall. She loves Mally devotedly—and she is talking very wildly."

The Earl glanced up sharply. "In what way?" he asked.

"Oh! Blaming herself for what has befallen. It is her 'sin' as she chooses to call it that is being punished. For my part I do not see how that can be so, else why should Mally's father, who is at least equally culpable, go scot free? But she seems to feel that she has added to the burden of her guilt by not having Mally baptised. I did not perfectly understand how that came about—she was rambling away to herself—but I gathered it was something to do with her father and the incumbent of the parish, who appears to be a very stiff-necked sort of clergyman, well versed in prophecies of hellfire and eternal damnation."

"Old Barnett? Yes—he would be. Why in heaven's name didn't the wench appeal to me? Derwent would have christened the poor little brat, just for the asking. Is it too late now? I could have him back here within the hour—no! I forgot. He's gone off to Coldstone. There's no resident priest there, so he visits regularly to do what he can, and won't be back until tomorrow."

Elizabeth was carefully pouring the milk into a mug. "You are very kind, my lord," she said, with such patent sincerity that the Earl felt positively embarrassed. "I wonder—I have heard, though I have never known it done—that when a child lies at the point of death, baptism may be administered by a lay person."

She looked up at him enquiringly, her eyes beseeching. It was plain to see which way her thoughts were trending. Had the situation been other than it was, the Earl's expression of sheer horror must have been comic. To a man of deep if inarticulate faith, the suggestion that he might be called upon to administer one of the Church's solemn sacraments was sacrilegious. Thrown completely off balance, he actually stammered. "D-do you mean—oh no! I could not. I am not fit."

She did not argue or seek to persuade him, merely bowing her head in submission to his scruples. After a moment he said uneasily, "Do you think I ought to offer? Indeed I would very much rather not," and in his diffidence he looked young and vulnerable as Elizabeth had never seen him, so that a rush of tenderness filled her heart.

"You must do as you think right," she said gently. "No one would expect you to perform such a solemn act unwillingly." She moved towards the stairway, explaining that she must take the milk to Lucy before it cooled.

But even as she began the steep ascent a dreadful, almost inhuman wailing assailed their ears. Elizabeth hastily put down the cup, gathered her skirts and fled up the stairs, the Earl following swiftly on her heels.

Lucy had flung herself face downward on the bed, her arms wrapped about the pitifully contorted body of the child. The eerie keening had broken into a storm of sobbing, and it was only with difficulty that Elizabeth was able to draw her away. The Earl bent over the sickbed. Too late, now, for human aid. Gently he straightened the twisted little body, wiped away the blood that had gushed from the child's nose, and drew up the sheet over the quiet face.

At the finality of this action Lucy began to struggle in Elizabeth's restraining arms, crying out that it was only a convulsion, that her baby wasn't dead, until she had sobbed herself into exhaustion and allowed Elizabeth to half lead, half carry her from the room.

It would be a long time before the misery of the journey to Anderley would fade from Elizabeth's mind. Lucy was quieter. It seemed as though her in-bred respect for the Earl prevented her from making too great an outcry in his presence. But now, it emerged, she was obsessed by the fear that her child would be denied the right to burial in consecrated ground because she had not been baptised. On and on went the hoarse monotonous voice, pleading, praying, then with a sudden twist of mood resigned and hopeless.

The Earl, fully engaged in the task of guiding his horses along shadowy lanes illuminated only by the feeble light of a watery moon, had no attention to spare, even if he caught the burden of Lucy's plaint. It fell to Elizabeth to soothe and comfort, and she felt herself sadly ill-equipped to do so. She dare not make a confident promise that all would be well, being quite ignorant of the law in such cases. At last, in desperation, she reminded Lucy of the story of Christ bidding His friends to let the children come to Him, and this at last seemed to bring the girl a measure of comfort, for surely a priest of Christ's Church would never go against so clear a command? The weary voice fell silent, save for an occasional plea for repeated reassurance. Elizabeth could only be thankful, for she felt that it was for wiser heads than hers to resolve the situation.

For the first time since she had been brought to Anderley she was unreservedly grateful for the standard of service and comfort that the Earl maintained. Though it was past three in the morning a groom was on the alert for his return, ready to take charge of the horses. A lamp was burning in the hall, and no less a person than the majestic Harrison himself came softly forward to attend to any wishes that his master might choose to express. A brief low-voiced colloquy ensued. The Earl turned to Elizabeth, who was standing wearily with one arm round the drooping Lucy.

"You will want to see her safely bestowed," he said gently. "I have asked Harrison to have Gertrude called. She is one of the maids with whom Lucy was friendly before she went away, and she is a kindly girl who will be glad to help her former friend. Once you have persuaded Lucy to swallow Dr Hartwell's draught, you may safely leave her to Gertrude's care. I think you should take some refreshment before you retire, for you must be quite exhausted. Harrison will bring wine and biscuits to the library and I beg that you will join me there when you have seen Lucy settled."

Elizabeth began to murmur something vague and disjointed about not being so *very* tired—she was not so poor a creature—and her gratitude for his concern, but the advent of Gertrude put an end to her protestations. Gertrude had obviously dressed by guess and in great haste. Her gown was buttoned awry and the hem of her nightgown hung an irregular inch below it, her cap had been crammed on hurriedly on top of her curling rags and she was still sleep-flushed and drowsy-eyed. But she hurried to Lucy's side full of kindly concern, and Lucy, too emotionally drained to be on the defensive, allowed herself to be led upstairs unresisting, borne on the floodtide of Gertrude's warm sympathy.

In the library the Earl waited patiently for Elizabeth's return beside a fire which Harrison had cunningly replenished with a double handful of fir cones and some small logs. On first coming into the room he had snuffed the candles, so that only the fireglow lit the semi-circle about the hearth, where a low chair had been set ready for Elizabeth with the tray standing on a tripod table beside it.

He leaned back lazily in his own chair, stretching his long limbs luxuriously, his body relaxed, his expression inscrutable as ever, until the door opened softly and Elizabeth appeared on the threshold and came rather diffidently towards him. Then he was on his feet in one swift movement, catching her cold hands to draw her to the comfort of the hearth and installing her in the easy chair with a reverence that would have graced a throne-room. She had taken time to tidy her hair and bathe her face and hands, but she looked pale and tired and her gown was hopelessly crumpled. Not even the devoted Miss Clara would have claimed that the beloved niece was in her best looks. To the Earl she seemed wholly lovable in her weariness. He was aware of an almost overmastering desire to take her in his arms and coax her back to confident happiness, coupled with a deep regret that this was definitely not the moment for such behaviour. Even setting aside the tragic experience that they had just shared, it would be highly improper for a guardian to be making love to his ward alone in a sleeping house at four o'clock in the morning. Impatient of convention the Earl might be, but his love should be treated with the honour due to a princess of the blood. So it was only the hint of reluctance with which he released her hands that might have betrayed him to an onlooker, had there been one.

"Indeed, my lord, I came only to tell you that Lucy has taken the draught and then to bid you goodnight," protested Elizabeth, as the Earl, without enquiring her preference, poured sherry into her glass.

"Nevertheless you will drink your wine and be the better for it," he said coolly, with a return to the old masterful manner, holding out the glass so that she was forced to take it from him just for good manners, and having done so found herself sipping it without conscious thought and then acknowledging that he had been right to insist. The mellow golden liquid eased a little of the ache of unshed tears in her throat, and the burden of helpless pity was insensibly lightened by the deep security that seemed to enfold her in the quiet firelit room. She found herself thinking sleepily that his lordship would know just what to do and that she could leave it all to him, and on the thought she smiled across at him with such open affection and trust that the Earl's hands closed sharply on the arms of his chair and he had to remind himself hastily of the good resolutions so recently made.

"You have been so kind to me tonight," she said dreamily, and he realised that in her weariness she was not so much talking to him as thinking aloud, "that it is hard to believe that I hated you so much at first."

The involuntary jerk of the Earl's head and the wry twist of his lips roused her to the knowledge that she had spoken aloud. She blushed rosily, but the tired blue eyes met his bravely enough, and she went on steadily, "That had to be said between us, my lord, though indeed I had not meant to say it at this present. But having begun, I will finish. Since I have come to reside under your roof you have shown me a kindness far beyond what was required of you by duty. I am deeply sensible of your care for me, and beg you to pardon any—any discourtesy that I may have shown before I learned to value you as I should."

Stem measures were called for, decided the Earl, or he would be catching the lovable penitent into his arms and smothering her with kisses. He pulled himself together firmly.

"Blackmailer and bullying tyrant—bloodstained brute—" he enumerated thoughtfully. "Would you call them discourtesies, Miss Kirkley? I shudder to think what terms you would regard as insults! But come, my child. It is *not* kind in me to tease you when you are so sleepy that you scarce know what you are saying. To bed with you. We will continue this discussion at a more suitable time."

Even in her present humble state of mind this was going too far. "I am *not* a child," she said with dignity, and would have gone on to aver that she knew very well what she was saying had not the Earl laid one finger lightly across her lips.

"Are you not?" he asked softly. "To me you seem a veritable infant—but a very wise one," he added hastily, placatingly, "and one to whom my thanks for this day's work shall be rendered in due form when she is less sleepy."

He led her firmly to the foot of the stairs, lit her bedroom candle and put it into her hand. Then he took her free hand into his and raised it to his lips, an action so unusual that even in her daze of exhaustion the blue eyes widened in surprise. The deep voice was so velvet soft—she could scarce believe that she had heard him aright, but must already be dreaming. He could not, surely, have said, "A beloved, adorable infant"?

Chapter Fourteen

Elizabeth woke late. The great house lay drowsing in its mid-day somnolence. She could hear the stable clock striking as she sat up in bed. Eleven o'clock already! Someone must have given orders that she was not to be wakened, and here was the morning almost spent and so much to be done. She jumped out of bed and pulled the bell to summon Edith, then drew back the curtains to let in the light of another grey day, with never a gleam of sun to raise one's spirits nor yet a drop of rain to bless the thirsty earth.

She turned to her wardrobe in search of a dress to lighten the prevailing gloom and cheer her own mood, for she felt unusually tense and restless this morning in spite of her long sleep. Part of her mind was mulling over the problem of Lucy and wondering what could be done to help her, but there were other thoughts clamouring insistently for attention. She wondered, safely enough, where her guardian was this morning and what he was doing, but then strayed on to the more dangerous and delightful ground of trying to recall his every word and expression during that brief and dreamlike interlude in the small hours. Edith, coming quietly into the room with a tray in her hands, found her mistress absently fingering the delicate crystal broidered gown that she had worn for the party, and exclaimed involuntarily, "Oh, no, Miss! Not for ordinary morning wear," in a tone so shocked that Elizabeth was sharply awakened from her idle dreaming.

"Of course not," she agreed. "I was just recalling that his lordship was pleased to approve this gown, but I had no thought of wearing it."

Edith set the tray on a table in the window. "His lordship gave orders that you were not to be disturbed this morning until you rang your bell, and then I was to bring you this. Which is why I was a bit long in coming, Miss, because I had to boil fresh water for the tea."

"Tea, at this hour?"

"The master's orders, Miss," said Edith, with a wooden countenance that betrayed more completely than obvious excitement her deep interest in these unusual proceedings. "He spoke to Mrs Abbot himself, and told her just what she was to send up, so better get back into bed, Miss, and drink your tea before it goes cold."

Elizabeth meekly did as she was bid, sunk in amazement over this new facet of her guardian's personality. Who would have dreamed that so essentially masculine a man would take thought for the small details of domestic comfort? There were new-baked scones on the tray, still warm in their napkin; and there was honey. Elizabeth smiled over that. She was indeed extremely partial to honey, a fact which had obviously been duly noted. "But he cannot have thought how sticky it would be, to eat honey in bed," she decided, spreading butter on her scone and stealing shy glances at a basket of nectarines, across the top of which was laid one glowing golden rose. She did not quite like to ask whether the rose had been Edith's own idea of making the tray look attractive, or whether it had been added by some other hand, and Edith volunteered no information on this interesting point. In the intervals of laying out fresh clothing for her mistress she said that Lady Hester had sent to tell her not to be worrying her head about Lucy Bassett. Lucy had benefited by a good long sleep, and was more composed this morning. It had been arranged that Gertrude should go back to the cottage with her and stay as long as she was needed.

"I would like to see Lucy before she goes," Elizabeth said, pouring out a second cup of tea. "Do you know when they are leaving?"

Early in the afternoon, Edith said, and went on to speak of the smallpox and how fortunate it was that the village had escaped. It seemed that the unfortunate pedlar who had brought the sickness to Bassett's cottage had been taking a short cut across the head of the dale and had never gone near the village itself.

"But to think of his lordship knowing all about the man dying, and never saying a word for fear of alarming folks," breathed Edith, who could never have kept so vital and dramatic a secret to herself for so much as five minutes. "Seems they were all prepared, though, if it did break out in the village. Everything was ready to turn the nursery wing into a fever hospital, if so be as it was needed."

Elizabeth did not answer. A great many puzzles were being made plain. This was why she had been forbidden the village—why Lady Hester had been preoccupied with just such stores as would be needed for setting up a hospital. She could not help feeling just a little sore at heart that she had not been admitted to the secret and allowed to help. But he had not known that she was safe from infection, and had not dared to ask. She had been just an added anxiety to his already heavy load.

Casually she picked up the rose, intent, apparently, on careful selection among the nectarines, all of which were equally perfect. "What a lovely rose!" she exclaimed with slightly artificial brightness, and waited hopefully. Alas! The rose, it transpired, from Edith's eager explanations, was a new one that Tom had only put in last year. This was its first flowering at Anderley. Elizabeth knew all about the growing attachment between her maid and the young under-gardener and she generally listened to the girl's enthusiastic tales of Tom's doings with sympathetic interest, but in this instance she could well have spared the details of all that Tom thought about this rose and several others. Edith took it for granted that it was Tom who had added the rose to the basket of fruit. Elizabeth, picturing sturdy snub-nosed Tom, with his freckled face and wide amiable grin, could not feel that he was capable of so poetic a gesture. She did not, of course, wish to think it. It was better that the rose should remain a mystery.

At least it helped her to a decision as to what she should wear. An insidious inner voice had been murmuring, "You do right to wear blue, Miss Kirkley," but she would not listen. Really, there was no need to take notice of a man's lightest word, just because one had been mistaken in one's first judgement of him.

"I'll wear the jonquil muslin with the velvet ribbons," she announced. "It will be cool, and the day promises to be uncommonly hot."

It was one of her prettiest afternoon dresses, beautifully cut but very simple, relying for its charm on the hundreds of tiny vertical tucks that formed the bodice from rounded bosom to tiny waist, and on the knots of velvet of a deeper shade of yellow which caught up the ruched hem rather naughtily into a series of shallow scallops which permitted a tantalising glimpse of dainty sandal and slim ankle.

"Yes, Miss!" said Edith, in a glow of approval, and spread the pretty thing with reverent fingers on the sofa which stood in one of the window embrasures. Elizabeth pushed aside the tray and carried the rose over to the light. Edith clasped her hands ecstatically. "Beautiful, Miss," she sighed. "Tucked into your sash? It's just the right colour! Let me make sure there are no thorns to catch in this delicate stuff," and she held out a hand for the flower which Elizabeth surrendered with a ridiculous sense of reluctance.

She lingered over her toilet, not quite sure that she was ready to leave the peaceful haven of her own room for the powerful emotional currents that might be awaiting her outside. If only she could be quite sure! When she was dressed at last and Edith had gone, she stood a little while longer gazing out on to the terrace below her window with unseeing eyes. It would be dreadful, quite unbearable, if she should have mistaken the affection that a guardian might quite properly bestow upon his ward for something deeper and sweeter. And she knew so little of men. Had he really said and meant the words that he had breathed over her hand last night? By today's grey light it seemed incredible.

The sound of voices in the garden caught her attention. The Earl was there with his steward, Burrows, evidently, from his explanatory gestures and Burrows's understanding nods, giving some kind of instructions. The two men walked on together to the end of the terrace and then separated, Burrows going off briskly in the direction of the main drive, the Earl descending the shallow steps that led to the sunken garden.

Her mind was made up. She would walk out of doors for a while and trust to chance for a casual encounter with her guardian. It would be easier to meet him so. There would be more room, as he himself would say, for manoeuvre. One could always break off a difficult conversation by pausing to admire a particularly fine blossom, or calling attention to a charming new aspect which one had noticed for the first time. Indoors was much more difficult. It would be too absurd to try to turn the subject by breaking suddenly into animated praise of the Van Dyck or the Rubens, even if one *had* been carefully instructed in all the proper things to say about them. She stifled a giggle at the ridiculous pictures conjured up by a fertile imagination, and went to put on her hat.

The Earl was not in the sunken garden when she finally strolled down the steps. *That* she had expected, since he did not care for formal gardens. For herself she rather liked its quaint air of precise order. The flower tubs were slightly over-ornamented, she decided critically, but with the fountain playing it would be a peaceful secluded spot to sit with one's sewing or a book; a safe place, too, for children to play. Here she blushed scarlet and shook her head vigorously in denial of such foolish imaginings. To be thinking of such things, just because an attractive man had whispered half-heard love words over her hand!

But suppose—just suppose! She perched herself on the rim of the silent fountain, slim feet dangling. Though the drought had broken at last there was still no water to spare for such pretty toys as fountains. An orange butterfly settled on her beribboned skirt and folded his wings. Perhaps the soft velvet had tricked him into believing that he had found a mate. She watched the creature idly, her mind still toying with 'suppose'. If he had really meant it, if she had heard aright, what would he say when they met again?

She pondered the thought deliciously, savouring its many possibilities. A man of his integrity would undoubtedly propose marriage if—again that horrid little word—he had been serious last night. But how? Not since schooldays had Elizabeth had access to those romantic novels so eagerly perused by young females who were carefully guarded from reality. Her memory of them was vague, and none of the noble heroes' stilted utterances sounded at all right as imagined from the lips of the Earl.

The butterfly flew away in disgust and a watery-looking sun crept out from behind its veil of clouds. She swung herself lightly to the ground and resumed her strolling progress, turning back towards the rose garden. She had a fancy to identify the bush from which her rose had been plucked. Her fingers gently enclosed the flower as she walked. And in the rose garden she came upon the Earl, but not, as she had hoped, alone. For Lucy was with him, bareheaded as though, catching sight of him from a window, she had run out of the house just as she was to speak with him. And clearly upon a matter of importance, for she was clasping his sleeve with both hands, her face lifted appealingly to his, her slight body tense with urgency. So absorbed were they in their talk that they had not noticed Elizabeth's approach, and instinctively she halted. There was such an air of intimacy between them that she felt like an intruder, and hesitated, uncertain whether to join them or to go back. And while she wavered the Earl put his hand over Lucy's clutching, pleading ones and said something which operated so powerfully upon the girl that she released her grip on his arm and stepped back, her whole pose incredulity incarnate. His decisive nod evidently confirming his words, Lucy caught his hand to her lips and kissed it passionately. Elizabeth, too far away to sense the embarrassment that he could not wholly dissemble at this blatant adoration, saw only that his free hand came up to touch the girl's dark head with gentle fingers. She waited for no more, but turned away and left them to finish their talk in privacy. Only yesterday the three of them had been linked together by a common task, a shared anxiety. Today she felt herself excluded. There was no place for her in this conclave.

She walked quietly back to the house, her mood of tremulous, half-eager anticipation dimmed to a vague, puzzled unhappiness. She did not understand its cause. There was a sore feeling in her breast and she felt lonely and unwanted. A wave of homesickness such as she had not felt for weeks seemed to overwhelm her with a longing for the clasp of Gran's loving arms and Aunt Clara's sturdy support, and it was only by a determined effort that she blinked back the tears. She bit her lips fiercely to stifle her vague yearnings with a sharper pain. A mean little voice inside her head suddenly made itself heard. "You're jealous," it said. "Because his tenderness was for Lucy—poor unhappy Lucy—you're whimpering like a lost puppy."

This was intolerable. The more so because it was, of course, the truth. But realising the true cause of one's miseries is at least one step along the road to fighting them, and instinctively she straightened herself. To be dawdling and dreaming here in the gardens would not help. She would go back to the house and find something to occupy her thoughts. As she crossed the terrace she was met by Miss Trenchard, who had been seeking her everywhere to enquire how she did after the trials of the previous day. Would she like to drive out for a little while? So *much* more restful than riding those excitable horses. They might even go as far as Little Cropton church, where there were some very unusual brasses to be seen, and a communion cup that dated back to the reign of Elizabeth.

In one way the suggestion was quite tempting, since, in her new mood, escape from Anderley seemed very desirable. But there was the question of bidding Lucy goodbye, and mention of this reminded Mary that Lady Hester had indeed said something about Lucy wishing to thank Miss Elizabeth for all her kindness before she went home. Perhaps it would be better if they planned their drive for tomorrow. That would give her time to search out the story of the Tudor chalice, for she believed that in an old volume in the library she had seen a reference to its having been given to the church by some long dead Anderley in memory of his sister, who had married the Lord of the Manor of Little Cropton and had subsequently borne him twenty-one children, of whom five sons and six daughters had survived to maturity.

Even to Elizabeth's unsettled spirits the gentle spinster's awed admiration for this feat of maternal endurance seemed mildly funny, and she was further soothed and steadied by her companion's placid monologue on the subject of ancient church plate, so that she went to bid Lucy farewell in a more equable frame of mind.

As it fell out there was no opportunity for conversation of an intimate or private nature since both Gertrude and Lady Hester were also present, the former a little flustered by her new importance, the latter calmly assuring herself that nothing had been left behind. Lucy seemed calm and resigned. Though sorrow had left its mark on pale face and tragic eyes and much weeping had roughened her soft voice, her thanks were spoken composedly enough with no trace of last night's desperate distress. Elizabeth ventured a tentative enquiry as to whether all the necessary arrangements had been made. "Yes, Miss," began Lucy, "his lordship—" but Lady Hester, speaking at the same time, finished the sentence for her. "His lordship has charged himself with that responsibility," she said repressively, and Elizabeth, realising that the subject must be a painful one for Lucy, said no more, but engaged herself to visit the girl within a few days. Lucy curtsied low and pressed Elizabeth's hand fervently. Then she was shepherded out to the waiting carriage by the vigilant Lady Hester with Gertrude fussing delightedly in attendance.

Elizabeth watched the carriage move off. It was a pity that the interview had been so cramped and stilted, but Lady Hester had seemed anxious to hurry the girl away. When next she went to visit her she would try, she decided, to revive the former interest in learning to read. That would give her thoughts a new direction and fill some of the lonely hours that would drag so painfully now that there was no Mally to care for. A little cheered by the thought of doing something practical to help Lucy, she turned to accompany Lady Hester back into the house.

That good lady, usually so amiable and garrulous, seemed oddly silent and reserved today, so that Elizabeth wondered if one of the beloved King Charles spaniels was ailing, but was assured upon enquiry that they were all in full health and spirits. Any reference to her darlings was generally sufficient to launch Lady Hester on an animated account of their latest antics, for she was perfectly convinced that her listener must share her own enthusiasm for such handsome, intelligent and lovable little creatures. Today she lapsed into a brooding silence, her placid brow creased by an unaccustomed frown, and presently announced with an abrupt change of subject that she was going to choose flowers to adorn the chapel. Elizabeth, thankful for any occupation that would serve to pass the hours of this seemingly interminable day, offered to help, and the two of them spent an invigorating half-hour in denuding garden and hot houses of some of their choicest blooms despite a spirited rearguard action by the head gardener.

They carried their plunder in triumph to the chapel, and Elizabeth went backward and forward filling the vases with fresh water while Lady Hester snipped away excess foliage and coaxed stubborn blooms into place. The chapel was cool and shadowy, its dimness lit only by narrow lancet windows which allowed the pale sunshine to cast faint overtones of scarlet and blue on the grey flagged floor. It was very quiet, the massively thick walls excluding all outside sounds. Elizabeth found herself stepping softly and hushing her voice to a whisper as though she might disturb the quiet dust that had lain for centuries in the family vaults below the flagstones. The chapel was not much used nowadays, most of the servants preferring to attend divine service in the village church, which made a pleasant little Sunday outing for them. Only on occasions of great family significance was it used for its original purpose. Fortunately Mr Derwent seemed to find sufficient scope for the exercise of his office in serving the needs of the lonely farms and hamlets which comprised much of the Anderley estate. He was another of the Earl's lame dogs, reflected Elizabeth with a tender little smile. Literally lame, too, for he had come to haven at Anderley after losing one foot as the result of a rock fall in a quarry accident. Called to bring spiritual comfort to a man hopelessly crushed and dying, a further slight fall had brought tragic consequences upon himself. He was always cheerful despite his handicap. He could still manage to sit a horse, the only means of reaching some of the remote cottages, though he had once wryly admitted to Elizabeth that his progress could scarcely be termed riding, any more than the sober quadrupeds especially provided for his use could properly be called horses.

Elizabeth set a vase of white roses on the altar. They were very lovely against the dark oak of the reredos and the air was already sweet with their scent, but for herself she would have preferred more colour and regretted that Lady Hester had chosen only white flowers.

"Just one more," said Lady Hester. "I think I will put this larkspur in the stone jar by the chancel steps, if you would be so good as to bring me some more water, my dear."

It was quite a step from the chapel to the rainwater butts that served this corner of the garden. Elizabeth did not hurry, carrying the water jug carefully to avoid splashing her muslin skirts. As she pushed open the heavy oaken door that guarded the chapel porch she heard voices and stopped involuntarily, wondering who was with Lady Hester, for it was

Lady Hester's voice that reached her, every syllable carrying perfectly on the quiet air.

"—absolute madness. What were you about to promise so outrageous a thing? I have carried out your wishes as regards the flowers in the chapel, but I cannot, for all my earnest endeavours, bring myself to acceptance. I beg of you, before it is too late, make some other arrangement. This one is unforgivable."

Elizabeth could not hear what was said in answer, for the speaker had his back to her, but there was no mistaking the Earl's deep tones. She set down the heavy jug, meaning to slip quietly away, but she was arrested in her flight. The Earl must have turned in her direction for now his words reached her clearly, gently spoken but with an underlying determination that would brook no opposition.

"I am truly sorry for your distress, Hester, but my promise is given and I intend to keep it. Derwent has agreed, and the burial will take place tomorrow. I do not see that it will cause the scandal you suggest. What should our neighbours care that I choose to bury this poor babe in our ancestral vault?"

This time it was Lady Hester's voice that was muffled to inaudibility, though the rising note of protest was plain to hear. The Earl's reply was brusque, and to Elizabeth, shattering.

"You are perfectly well aware that the child is as much a Scorton as you are. It is scarcely her fault that she was born out of wedlock. By blood she is as much entitled to her place in these vaults as you or I—and probably more so than several who lie here behind their smug memorial tablets with far less claim than Mally to Scorton blood," he added cynically.

Chapter Fifteen

Elizabeth could never clearly recall how she had reached her own room. Shocked to the heart by the secret that she had accidentally discovered, she must yet have retained sufficient instinct of self-preservation to effect her retreat in silence and then have fled to shelter and privacy, but all she could remember afterwards was the sharp click of the lock as she turned the key and then, flinging herself face down on the bed, breathless and shaking, her hands pressed over her ears as though to shut out those words that still seemed to be echoing across the quiet chapel. "She is as much a Scorton as you or I. It is not her fault that she was born out of wedlock."

She lay huddled, rigid, her breath coming in deep shuddering sobs while her dazed brain assimilated the shocking truth. There could be no evasion. It would have to be faced and accepted. So many small details were falling into place that it was impossible to delude oneself with the false hope of mistake or misunderstanding. Lucy's comfortable circumstances, Lady Hester's dismay on hearing of her own visit to the cottage, Timothy's shocked refusal to go there and his subsequent criticism of his uncle's conduct in allowing Lucy to live at home, all were explained. Even Mally's resemblance to someone whom she had never quite succeeded in identifying was now all too easy to trace. Little wonder that the Earl had been willing to render Lucy all possible service when it was his own child who lay dying.

And she had thought him disinterestedly kind, and had admired him wholeheartedly for his humanity! In her blind ignorance she had thought herself in love with him, had prayed that her love might be returned. Bitterly she recalled the shy dreams that she had indulged only this morning, and pounded the pillows with furious fists in her angry humiliation. It was pain beyond belief that she had been so easy a victim to the wicked charm that had seduced Lucy, and doubtless many another, to their own undoing.

At least she could be thankful that she had discovered the truth in time, before she had betrayed her folly for his amusement. If her heart was sick and sore, he should never guess. And it was at this point that the knowledge was born in upon her that she could not, would not, endure to meet him again. Some means of escape must be devised, and that immediately. She got up, and paced the room, planning, rejecting first one idea then another. She could not go home. That was the first place where he would seek her. But at least she had money in her purse—enough, she thought, to pay for a modest lodging for two or three nights—and when that was done there were things that she could sell. There was the diamond necklace, for instance. It had been bought by her father, a gift for his wife, in readiness to greet her own arrival into the world. The lovely delicate jewel, still in its faded velvet case, had been handed over to her as part of her inheritance. She had never worn it—probably, now, she never would—but it would fetch a considerable sum, enough, she hoped, to support her until she could think of some way of earning her own livelihood. Moreover it could be slipped into a pocket, and that was important, for if she was to escape she would have to ride for the first stage of the journey and it would be impossible to carry much with her.

It would also be extremely difficult to steal a horse, and quite impossible, she suddenly realised, to steal a saddle, for the harness room was kept locked, and several of the stable lads slept in the snug quarters above it and would certainly rouse at any amateurish attempts at forcing an entry. Very well, then, she would ride out openly instead of slipping away by night as she had first planned. She could probably still count on two or three hours' freedom from pursuit. Not as much as she would have wished, but it would have to suffice. And though it was rather late in the day to be setting out for a ride, she would go now. She could think of some excuse, and she dreaded that any moment a message might summon her to wait upon her guardian in the library. He had said that he would thank her in form for her efforts on Mally's behalf, and he was punctilious about such matters. He would not forget.

Hastily she unlocked the lacquered cabinet in which she kept her modest jewellery, took the necklace from its case and rolled it in a handkerchief, slipping it, together with her purse, under the maltreated pillows. Then she rang for Edith and bade her send a message to the stables.

"For I have the headache a little," she explained in languid tones so far removed from her usual manner that had Edith been just a little older she might have found them suspect. Instead she was all solicitude, suggesting that a rest upon her bed with Edith to bathe the poor head with sweet water of Cologne would be much more sensible. Elizabeth was firm. Fresh air was the only remedy that would serve. The girl departed reluctantly and Elizabeth sighed her relief. So far, so good.

She ripped off the sadly crumpled jonquil muslin and tossed it on the bed. A bruised and wilted yellow rose dropped from the velvet sash. She stared at it, deep unhappiness clouding her eyes. Then she picked it up, crushed the limp petals between her fingers, and hurled the shattered remnants into the empty fireplace.

The old-fashioned pocket to tie about her waist under her petticoat was the next need. Gran had bestowed it upon her to use when travelling, explaining the risk of being robbed in crowded public places. In sheltered luxury under the Earl's care she had never had cause to wear it, but it would serve a useful purpose now. Into it went purse and jewels, she tied the yellowing tapes securely, then hastily pulled on her riding habit to conceal the betraying evidence of intended flight. She was only just in time, for here was Edith back again, still disapproving and now distinctly cross also, since her mistress had made shift to change her dress without assistance. She did not quite dare to voice her reproaches, confining herself to sulky silence as she twitched the hurriedly donned habit into its proper folds and buttoned the tightly fitting sleeves with an air of gross ill-usage. Elizabeth, in a fever to be off, strove to keep rigid control over her voice and movements. No hint of her desperate urgency escaped her as Edith took out her hat with infuriating slowness, stopping to re-curl the ostrich feather which nestled under its downswept brim and to brush off one or two specks of invisible dust. She crammed it on over wildly ruffled locks, driving Edith at last to verbal remonstrance.

"Shall I not dress your hair again, Miss?" she asked.

Elizabeth could have screamed. Instead she said with an ill-assumed indifference, "Later. It would only make my headache worse to have you tugging at it now."

This was the final straw. Edith coloured furiously, bitterly hurt at this unkind aspersion on her skill, and retreated in dignified fashion to the door, pausing at the last moment to say sullenly, "I gave your message to Robert, Miss, seeing as how Jacky had gone off to his mother's, him not thinking you'd be wanting to ride so late in the day."

Elizabeth nodded absently, scarcely aware of the girl's going, still less of her hurt feelings. The first, most critical stage of the adventure was upon her, and all her mind was bent on effecting her escape from the house without encountering her guardian. In the event she met no one at all as she made a carefully negligent descent of the main staircase and strolled across the south front of the house to the covered way that seemed to promise sanctuary. She met with the first slight set-back in the stable yard. In the absence of her own special groom, young Robert, the latest recruit to the staff, had saddled Jackstraw. And Jackstraw was not the mount she would have chosen for this enterprise. Robert's choice was natural enough. She had several times ridden the horse, an interesting ride when one could give him the whole of one's attention, but quite unreliable. It was true that he had an amazing turn of speed and a very comfortable action, but he also had less engaging qualities. However, there was no time now for useless regrets. She settled herself in the saddle, dealt patiently with the display of temperament with which Jackstraw always favoured his rider on being mounted, and held him down with some difficulty to the gentle trot permissible to a young lady with a headache.

It was a relief when, turning in the saddle, she realised that Anderley was out of sight and could allow Jackstraw to lengthen his stride. She had not been able to plan the next stage of her journey with accuracy, for she had no idea of the timing of the mail coaches along the Keighley-Kendal turnpike, although she knew that there was a posting house in Kirkby Lonsdale and thought that the mails also stopped there. If she could obtain overnight lodging for herself at the Rose and Crown, and stabling for the horse until such time as he could be returned to his owner, she would take the first coach on the following morning. She hoped it would be a north-bound vehicle since she was less likely to be sought in that direction, but north or south she would put as much distance as she could between herself and Anderley.

Now that she was safely set upon the road to freedom she fell into a fit of the dismals. Her action had cut her off entirely from family and friends. For the first time in her life she had only herself to depend upon, and she had no idea how long she might have to remain in hiding and still less about how to set about disposing of a valuable diamond necklace. That she might have to face worse difficulties, that her appearance and actions might attract the attention of the curious to a most uncomfortable degree, never entered her head. For most of her much vaunted twenty-three years she had occupied a humble station in life, inconspicuous and disregarded. It did not occur to her that for a young lady of obvious wealth and breeding, beautifully dressed but quite unattended and without baggage, there might be difficulty in remaining concealed for so much as a day, especially when the young lady was riding the Earl of Anderley's Jackstraw, almost as well known in the district as his noble owner.

Her thoughts dwelt wistfully on Gran and Aunt Clara, and she wondered how she could set their minds at rest as to her safety. But it must be several days before the news of her disappearance could reach them and perhaps by then she would have contrived some means of sending a message. And on one point at least she was perfectly confident. She had no fears for their well-being. Even in her present state of revulsion from her guardian, she judged him too proud a man to seek revenge for her flight on two innocent old ladies.

Jackstraw, becoming aware of the slack hands on the reins, made a spirited attempt to snatch the bit and take control, and only her instinctive horsemanship saved the runaway from the final indignity of being run away with. At the same moment she felt a few drops of rain on her cheek and looked up in dismay at the lowering clouds. With so much else to think about she had taken no heed of the weather. The flurry of drops died away and she breathed a prayer that the rain would hold off for an hour or two yet, since she had no desire to arrive at the Rose and Crown soaked to the skin.

She had made good speed in spite of her preoccupation. The turnpike road which cut across this distant corner of Anderley land was already in sight, deserted save for a solitary horseman riding slowly towards her. Some farmer on a fat old cob coming back from market, she thought idly, and then, heart plunging in utter dismay, recognised the rider. No farmer, but the Earl of Anderley's chaplain, returning from one of his pastoral visits.

Above all she must not arouse any suspicion. With racing pulses she rode steadily on. All was not yet lost. Certainly Mr Derwent would carry news of her to Anderley, and when the hue and cry was raised he would be able to give the pursuit a good lead. But no one would know whether she had turned north or south along the turnpike, and in any case it would take the poor man a couple of hours to reach Anderley, even if he tried to make haste. In that time, on Jackstraw, she could be miles away.

She greeted the chaplain in friendly fashion, and though he expressed mild surprise at seeing her so far from home on such a threatening day, he did not appear unduly suspicious, merely enquiring if she meant to ride much farther since he feared the rain was now threatening in earnest. Just to the turnpike, she told him, thankful that there could be no question of riding in company. Jackstraw was already fretting impatiently, dancing and sidling as was his custom when kept waiting. She would have liked to urge him at once to his utmost speed but it was more important to ensure that Mr Derwent was out of sight before she reached the road, while to make off at a furious gallop would do nothing to establish the innocent nature of her excursion. So she held the fidgety Jackstraw to a strict trot, saluted the chaplain with her whip, and left him to resume his plodding homeward progress.

The turnpike reached, she reined in and feigned admiration of a remarkably dull view in order to scan the countryside in all directions. Nothing moved. Mr Derwent had disappeared from sight. With a sigh of relief she turned her horse's head to the north and indicated with hand and heel that he might now show what he was made of. He accepted the invitation with enthusiasm and fled down the grassy verge at racing speed. It was like nothing so much as flying, thought Elizabeth, the wild exhilaration of sheer pace momentarily drowning all other sensations. She murmured soft encouragement to the powerful black, and at the same instant felt the saddle slipping.

It was one of his favourite tricks—puffing himself out when he was being saddled so that the girths were not taken up properly. Young Robert had not noticed, and she, in her distraction, had for once forgotten to test the girths. With every art at her command she sought to check the headlong speed and did indeed succeed in moderating it, but it was too late. She was completely off balance, and a sharp bend in the road accomplished the inevitable. The black veered to the right, the saddle slipped around under his belly, and Elizabeth was thrown clear. It was fortunate for her that a bed of tough, springy heather took the worst force of the impact. She fell on the point of her left shoulder, and at the same time took a stunning blow on the head from a boulder that lay hidden among the heather roots. It was some time before she struggled back to consciousness, aware first of fierce pain in her head, and then, as she put up a hand to investigate, that her shoulder, too, had suffered in the fall, while the force of it had thrust her deep into the heather where the sharp sprigs and protruding roots had torn her hands and face and then closed over her, so that in her present weak and battered state they were holding her a prisoner. A groan of mingled pain and helplessness broke from her as she realised the full extent of her predicament, and she struggled as best she could to free herself from her heathery prison, but the tough roots had actually pierced the fabric of her habit and were literally holding her pinned to the ground. Her efforts only made her sick and dizzy, and presently she subsided limply, a few tears of desperation trickling weakly down her scratched and dirty face.

To add to her miseries it began to rain again, a steady relentless downpour which soon soaked through her habit and chilled her to the bone. She was not above fifteen yards from the road but only two vehicles passed, both southbound, their drivers well muffled against the rain, and her cries for help were lost in the clatter of wheels and hoofs. Soon the growing murk of dusk and overcast would make her invisible. She tried once more to pull herself erect, the better to call attention to her plight, but the useless struggle caused her such intense pain that she fainted.

It was full dark when she roused again, but between pain and exposure she was only half conscious. There were lights dancing and floating in the darkness, and she fancied she could hear voices. She tried to call again, but the husky little croak that resulted was barely audible. She gathered her failing strength to try once more, and this time with better fortune. There was a sharp exclamation. She heard the clatter of boots on the metalled road and one of the lanterns moved steadily in her direction as a voice called out, "There's something or someone here—I heard a kind of cry— but I don't know if—" At which point the rescuer tripped over a root, put out a hand to save himself, and clutched a handful of wet velvet. A moment's hasty inspection sufficed. Then a triumphant yell went up. "She's here! I've found her."

Vaguely she was aware of more lanterns converging on her. The lights dazzled and hurt. It was easier to lie with eyes closed. A gruff voice called out something about sending a message to the other parties and someone stooped and tried to lift her. Pain shot through the injured shoulder so that she cried out, though feebly, and lapsed into insensibility once more.

*

She was aware of a soft rosy glow, and of shadows passing between herself and the source of this light. There was a murmur of lowered voices, and then one, clear and incisive, that compelled her attention even in her drowsy state.

"She will do well enough now. Sleep will be her best doctor. Do you stay here with her, Ruth, and keep some of the broth hot against her awakening. I will go tell my brother and Lord Anderley that she is in no present danger."

Another, lower, voice made some remark that Elizabeth did not catch.

"I had forgotten," said the first speaker. "Lock it away safely in my jewel box. Lord Anderley will not want to be bothered with it tonight. The purse you may leave on the dressing chest." There was the sound of a door opening and closing gently, and then soft noises indicative of someone setting a room to rights—the chink of china, and the sound of water being poured away. Presently even these ceased, and save for the hiss and crackle of the flames, silence reigned.

Elizabeth lay drowsily wondering where in the world she was now, but not greatly concerned. She was floating placidly on a sea of lethargy, and the snatch of conversation that she had heard had allayed some anxiety deep buried in her mind, even though she could not have said just what it was. Soothed, warmed and reassured, she fell asleep.

Some time in the night she awakened to a greater awareness of her surroundings and a consuming thirst. She was lying in an enormous four-poster bed with the curtains drawn only part way round it so that she could both see and be seen. There was a fire burning on the hearth and someone wrapped in a shawl sitting beside it, someone who rose at the sound of movement from the bed and came softly towards her.

"Art thee awake, dearie?" said a warm country voice. "Never fret. Thee's safe and with friends. Thee suffered a nasty fall, and they carried thee here to the nearest shelter. See now, let me raise the pillow a little and then I will fetch thee a drink. Art parched, I vow." She went back to the hearth and turned up a lamp that had been burning low. "I've some good broth here that will set thee up finely," she offered. But Elizabeth begged for a drink of water and gulped it greedily, gazing with startled eyes over the rim of the glass at the vast chamber in which she lay. Never in all her life had she seen anything like it. Firelight and lamplight illuminated scarce a quarter of its length. Massive furniture caught the light and returned a gleam here and there from the shadows, and the one wall that she could clearly see was hung with a magnificent tapestry of a hunting scene, while the chimney piece above the cavernous stone fireplace was carved with some heraldic device. She had not thought that such apartments existed outside the pages of a history book. Eyes round as a young owlet's, she held out the glass to be refilled and said timidly, "Pray tell me, ma'am, whose house is this?"

Her kindly nurse smiled at her. "Not ma'am to me, child," she said gently. "My name is Ruth, and I'll be glad to have thee use it. This is

Greystocks." And as Elizabeth still stared at her blankly added in explanation, "The Marquis of Ecclesfield's country seat."

That brought reassurance. She remembered the pleasant lad at the party who had squired her so competently and insisted that her guardian should bring her to visit him. Neither of them had expected the visit to be paid in these circumstances, but it was comfortable to feel that she had fallen in with a friend.

Ruth was pouring broth into a bowl and insisting that she should try to swallow a little. It was easier to submit though she was not in the least hungry, and it was very strange to be spoonfed like a baby. Meekly she accepted almost as much as Ruth thought desirable, but was thankful to be allowed to sink back into the pillows and told to go to sleep again. As the motherly hands tucked the covers close about her she asked sleepily, "Are all the bedchambers as huge as this one?" And Ruth laughed at her and assured her that indeed they were not. This was one of the state apartments, but Master Hugh—for at times she was apt to forget her former nurseling's present dignities—had declared that a lady with so royal a name must be royally housed. And on this encouraging note of homage she slipped over the borders of sleep.

Chapter Sixteen

The week that Elizabeth passed at hospitable Greystocks never seemed quite real to her. She had a sense of standing outside herself, surveying her own activities with an onlooker's detachment. For the first day she was aware only of her own aches and pains and the vast amount of trouble to which she was putting her host and hostess. By the second, good nursing and her own youth and resilience had largely mended the ailing body, and any idea that she could possibly be a nuisance had been laughed out of court. It almost seemed that the Marquis and Lady Ann could have no engagements of their own, so wholly did they devote themselves to the entertainment of their uninvited guest. When she protested that she was taking up too much of their time, Lady Ann assured her that she was a veritable honey fall, supplying the one amenity that Greystocks lacked—congenial feminine company. "Hugh told me that I should like you," she said, "and indeed I do. I mean to keep you here as long as I can. When you are fully recovered there are a thousand things I want to show you."

From the appearance of the state bedroom it would seem that she had already made a good beginning. Its serene dignity had been sadly overlaid by all the clutter indispensable to the hobbies and amusements of lively young people. The invasion had begun respectably enough with books, periodicals and fashion journals. But when it was found that too much reading gave Elizabeth a headache, other entertainment must be sought. Ann, digging joyfully into the treasure house of her schoolgirl days, brought out shell work and brightly coloured papers for the construction of flower mosaics. Cards, chessmen, draughts and a backgammon board appeared—and took up residence. And when Elizabeth was allowed to get up and the Marquis was admitted to the feminine conventicle, the collection was further augmented by all the paraphernalia required by a fertile and inventive imagination for the tying of flies. Hugh had recently acquired one of the modern fishing rods fitted with a reel so that the line could be paid out or wound in as required, and though his sister assured him that any self-respecting salmon would turn in disgust from the current creation of tinsel and gaudy feathers, he only retorted cheekily that fish

109

were possessed of a curiosity almost feminine, and would swallow anything, so it were dressed up pretty enough.

The easy camaraderie between brother and sister was a new experience for Elizabeth, but so frank and friendly were their manners that it was not long before she was joining in the battle of wits and words on equal terms and generally giving as good as she got. So the days passed pleasantly enough, even gaily.

It was only in the night watches when she could not sleep after the day's unaccustomed idleness that her mind was troubled by the problem that had driven her from Anderley and that still remained unsolved, if not, indeed, further complicated by her own hasty action in running away. It was difficult to decide whether those at Anderley had discovered her true purpose. Certainly it was not mentioned the first time that Lady Hester and Mary drove over to visit her, and though their silence on this occasion might have been attributed to consideration for her invalid state, surely something would have been said now that she was definitely convalescent? She had fully expected to be taken to task and asked to explain herself, a prospect which made her feel quite sick. Instead, once Lady Hester was assured that she was well on the road to recovery, she had been mildly triumphant over so complete a vindication of her views on the dangers of riding alone, and clearly assumed that this reprehensible practice would now be forbidden when Elizabeth came home. She gave no least hint, by word or manner, that there might be anything awkward about that homecoming.

Elizabeth took what comfort she could from the thought that there had really been nothing to betray her intention except the diamond necklace which now lay safely locked in Ann's jewel box. If Ann thought it was an odd sort of thing to carry with one on a country ride she was too well bred to show any surprise, merely assuring Elizabeth of its safety and agreeing to keep it for her until she went home. It seemed probable that no one else except Ruth knew anything about it.

On one point, however, Ann did not trouble to conceal her growing interest and curiosity. It had seemed natural enough that each morning should bring some small gift—a basket of fruit or a book or magazine from Anderley, though to be sure there were enough and to spare of such comforts at Greystocks. But it was not long before Ann noticed that though there was never a card or a note with these offerings they were always accompanied by one solitary yellow rose. It was apparent to the meanest intelligence that there must be a hidden significance in this flower, and Ann would have dearly loved to know the secret. She took to covertly studying Elizabeth's expression when she received the daily tribute, but Elizabeth had already schooled herself to an indifferent setting aside of the flower, and her reception of the gifts was polite rather than rapturous.

Ann could only surmise that they must come from Timothy Elsford, perhaps already wearying of little Miss Bentley, and she was not at all sure that she approved, for though she liked Timothy well enough as a gay and amusing companion, she did not feel that he was a good match for Elizabeth. Yet the only other eligible male residing at Anderley was Mr Derwent, and though *him* she valued highly, he was not a man whom one associated with the more romantic forms of courtship.

Elizabeth had been allowed to come downstairs and Lady Hester was beginning to drop hints that it was time for her to be thinking of a return to Anderley when Ann carried the square package into the Ladies' Parlour one morning. Elizabeth glanced up from the journal she was reading and Ann fancied that her colour deepened a little, but could not be quite sure. She turned away tactfully, busying herself with collecting a scatter of rose petals that had fallen on the polished mahogany but hearing all the while the rustle of the paper as Elizabeth unwrapped it. Presently a puzzled voice said, "Look at this, Ann! Do *you* know what it is? For I'm sure I've never seen anything like it before."

Ann looked—and drew a startled breath. Elizabeth was holding a curiously carved ball of green jade. With creditable self-possession Ann put aside the incredible revelation that had just been vouchsafed her and answered as calmly as her inner excitement would permit, "It's a puzzle; a Chinese ball. See—it takes to pieces. And there is one key piece that holds all the rest together. We have one ourselves, made in ivory, that my grandfather brought back from his travels in the East. This one—"—there was the briefest possible hesitation as she swiftly changed the sentence—"Goodness! It must have been made for an Emperor's son! See how beautifully it is carved, and how smoothly the sections fit together. It's a real treasure. You lucky, lucky girl!"

The last words came out with unfeigned sincerity, and did not refer to the gift of the jade ball. For Ann had seen that ball before, and once, on her tenth birthday, had been permitted to handle it. There could be no mistaking it, or its giver. And the gift of so rare and costly a bauble could mean only one thing.

Bubbling with suppressed excitement, she chattered away almost at random, blandly assuring her friend that she might perfectly properly accept the gift, that its value lay in its beautiful workmanship and that it was no more personal than, say, a pretty fan or a bouquet holder, and longing all the time to get away and find Hugh, to share with him the secret that she had discovered. But when she eventually succeeded in running him to earth in the gun-room his reaction to her disclosures was rather disappointing.

"Anderley and Elizabeth? Yes. I had a notion there was something like that in the wind. I should think it will do very well. You like it, too, don't you?"

"Yes, of course I do. Nothing could be better. To have Elizabeth for our close neighbour, and Anderley opened up again as it was used to be. Why on earth didn't you tell me your suspicions sooner?"

Hugh looked vaguely uncomfortable. "Nothing really to go on," he said gruffly. "Just the way he looked at her—sort of proud and anxious, like Starlight with her foal. But I wasn't sure about her. Dash it, Ann, I'm not a girl, to be noticing sighs and becks and languishings. She seemed to like him well enough, but more than that I wouldn't care to stake my blunt on. There's been nothing announced, nor even hinted, and what's more he's not been once to visit her this sennight. Something damned odd about that, specially if you'd seen the stew he was in over her accident. Better not refine too much on what may turn out to be nothing but a hum."

"But Hugh! The Chinese ball! He would never have sent her *that* if his intentions had not been serious. You know how the Anderleys venerate the thing. I'm sure I must have heard the story a dozen times—how it is supposed to signify completion and perfection, and, that if one holds the secret of the key piece one holds the world in one's hand. I do not know how I kept myself from telling her that the thing was as good as a proposal of marriage. But she seemed so cool, so unaware."

"Aye—and there's the rub," her brother grunted. "Richard's serious enough. But I told you. I couldn't be sure about her."

Ann's face grew sober, even troubled. "Oh dear! Surely no girl in her senses could resist Richard if he was in earnest? If I did not adore my own darling Malcolm I vow I could be in love with him myself. He is so perfectly one's notion of the chivalrous knights of old. But now that you speak of it, *I'm* not sure of her either. She has never paid the least heed to his gifts. She cannot have sent him a note, or I must have known of it. And

Hugh! I greatly fear that when she came by that fall she was running away. Though the matter has not been discussed between us, she was carrying a diamond necklace in a concealed pocket. Ruth and I found it when we undressed her. Why else should she do so, unless to turn it into money?"

No normal brother could immediately concede that his sister might be right. "Could have had some sentimental association I suppose—didn't want to be parted from the thing—always carried it with her—gift from some other fellow," suggested the Marquis helpfully.

His sister was suitably shocked. "No honourable man would give so costly a gift except to his wife," she assured him, and, at his sudden grin, "Very well, then, or to his—his fancy piece. And then he wouldn't be an honourable man to my way of thinking. But in any case it's no such thing, for the necklace is quite old fashioned—the stones of good quality but the setting antiquated—much more like a family heirloom than a love token."

Neither of the serious young creatures wasted a thought on how many love tokens must in time become dull and antiquated family heirlooms, nor dreamed of the tragedy that lay behind this one. They were concerned only with the odd behaviour of their friends.

"Is there nothing at all that we can do, then?" begged Ann, after further fruitless discussion.

Hugh shook his head. "Best not to meddle. Leave it to Richard. If anyone can bring the thing off, he can."

Ann went slowly back to the Ladies' Parlour, where Elizabeth, for once forgetting the giver in the gift, was absorbedly endeavouring to fit the pieces of the jade ball together. She looked up, her face bright and amused. "It's a maddening thing," she protested. "I've been trying and trying and I just can't get it right."

Ann smiled absently and picked up the neglected rose that had, as usual, accompanied the gift. "It's just a knack," she said. "One must get the key piece right. Then it's easy." She hesitated a moment, then said, "This is a gorgeous rose, Elizabeth. What is it called?"

The bright animation faded from Elizabeth's face. "I don't know if it has a name," she said quietly. "Be a darling and put this thing together for me, Ann, or I shall fritter away the whole morning over it. Oh! And there's a letter for you on the secretaire. Ruth brought it in just now. The man had forgotten it."

Ann picked up the note and opened it. It was brief and casual. The writer trusted that it would be convenient for her to receive him that afternoon.

He understood from his sister that his ward was now sufficiently recovered to return to her home, and would give himself the pleasure of driving over to Greystocks to collect her, and, at the same time, of thanking his friends for their care of her.

She glanced beneath her lashes at Elizabeth's head, bent over the pieces of jade in her lap. "Oh dear!" she said, softly, ruefully. "What a shame to snatch you away so soon. Lord Anderley writes that he is coming for you this afternoon. I had hoped that he would have spared you to us for longer." And then chattered on about the things that she had planned to do, and how they must meet again very soon, whether at Anderley or at Greystocks. For Elizabeth had raised a face so white and shocked at the simple news that Ann realised that here was something far beyond her understanding. She knelt beside Elizabeth and took the pieces of jade from her shaking fingers, fitting them together with the ease of intimate acquaintance.

"There you are—see? Simple! I told you—it's just a matter of the key piece being right."

Elizabeth looked at the beautiful thing as the vital section slid into place and locked home and Ann laid it on her lap. "Yes," she said quietly, in a strange, dead sort of voice, as though, Ann reported later to her brother, she was talking in her sleep. "If the key piece is right, then everything else falls into place. But what if it isn't, Ann? What if it is flawed or broken?" And then, before Ann could puzzle out her meaning, she laughed—a hard, false little laugh—and said, "Pray take no notice of my nonsensical talk. I really begin to wonder if that knock on the head has affected my intellect. If his lordship is indeed coming for me this afternoon I must see to my packing, for it will never do to keep him waiting."

Chapter Seventeen

So long as they were at Greystocks it was all very much easier than had seemed possible. Hugh and Ann vied with one another in greeting the Earl with an affectionate teasing warmth that glossed over Elizabeth's stiffer reception, and by the time she had received, instead of an anxious enquiry into her health, the Earl's considered opinion on people who let go the rein for a mere tumble, and had defended herself with spirit by animadverting on people who kept in their stables animals with no more manners than a costermonger's donkey, the depraved monster of her recent imaginings had vanished. Despite all the weight of evidence against him her loving heart refused to believe that this man had compassed the ruin of one of his own dependents. Reason might insist that this was the truth, but instinct defied evidence. She could not help responding to the laughter in the grey eyes, the affection underlying the teasing, and the protective strength of the hand that was so swift to steady her when she chanced to stumble. It could not last, of course. She could not for ever close her eyes to the truth. But just for a little while she would yield to the temptation to sun herself in his presence. So she sustained her part in the gay quartet quite adequately, and neither the Earl, who had preoccupations of his own, nor Ann, who was watching her closely, suspected anything amiss, or guessed that the cheerful veneer was perilously thin.

Departure from Greystocks was naturally delayed. The Earl must be dragged off to the home pasture to see Starlight's foal, and then on to the west paddock to give his opinion on Ann's new hack. Then, amid much laughter, Hugh must show him Elizabeth's lamentable attempts at paper mosaics which Ann declared to be almost as bad as Hugh's salmon flies. The Earl, solemnly studying his ward's creations through his glass, deprecated their flimsy construction but suggested that Hugh might try their lure if all else failed. They would certainly startle the salmon. But he added earnestly that such an unorthodox method of stunning the wily fish was perhaps hardly sporting. That led quite naturally to the rapidly improving water situation and the prospect of better sport. Then Ann insisted that they must all take tea before she could allow the invalid to face the rigours and privations of an hour's drive, and over tea the men fell into discussion of how far the recent drought was likely to affect the shooting season. By the time that they had agreed that the prospects were better than anyone could reasonably have hoped, the afternoon was gone and the Earl was saying that they must be away before the cool of the evening since he had brought the phaeton rather than a closed carriage, thinking that on so lovely a day Miss Kirkley would enjoy the fresh air.

The barefaced impudence of this remark caused Ann to bite back a smile. To be sure the day was mild enough, nor was it actually raining. But the impression created of blue skies and smiling sunlight was sheer fantasy. A man who could utter such a prevarication without so much as a blink deserved to win his way, she thought in silent salute, for no one ventured to demur, or to suggest that there were plenty of alternative vehicles available. Ann, at any rate, had a shrewd notion that the phaeton had been deliberately chosen for the drive to ensure that there could be no eavesdroppers.

Even when Hugh helped her up into the phaeton and the Earl swung himself into the driving seat, Elizabeth was not aware of any undue awkwardness, for Ann was still talking about their next meeting and enquiring whether she would not wear a thicker pelisse, or even a shawl to wrap about the bruised shoulder. It was not until they drew out of the gates of Greystocks and on to the turnpike that the paralysing dumbness descended upon her. In every fibre of her being she was intensely aware of the man beside her, and she could not think of a single thing to say that might dispel the rising tension between them. She sat with down-bent head, fidgeting with a glove which she had pulled off just for the relief of having something to do with her hands and still deeply conscious of the muscular thigh in well-worn buckskin so close to hers, and the gleaming boot that dwarfed her delicate slipper. She tried to fix her attention on the beautifully matched bays, only to focus on capable brown hands managing the reins with careless precision and indicating with the whip the place where she and Jackstraw had parted company.

"At least you had the good sense to pick the heather," commented the laconic voice. "Further on it's mostly limestone paving."

She seemed quite unable to make a reply, even to so harmless a remark as this. The Earl glanced down at her and said, with a hint of laughter in his voice, "You are unusually silent, Miss Kirkley. I hope you do not mean to pick a quarrel with me because I teased you about your flower mosaics?"

She managed to force a stiff little smile and a shake of the head, whereupon the deep gentle voice went on, "Because I have a favour to ask of you, and I thought this might be a propitious moment."

Still no reply. She did not even dare to venture an enquiring glance, but waited with wildly beating heart and fingers clenched on the crumpled glove for what he would say.

"Hearing you on such easy terms with Ann and Hugh, it seems to me that I, too, might now be granted the privilege of calling you by your given name."

She breathed a little sigh of relief, though she scarcely knew what she had feared.

"May I, Elizabeth?" he urged gently, and a husky little voice managed at last to say, "Yes, my lord, if you wish."

He thanked her gravely, and for the moment said no more. He had never previously proposed marriage, but of late he had given a good deal of thought to the subject, and had decided that to undertake so delicate a business while his hands were fully occupied in managing his horses would be foolish in the extreme. If literary precedent were to be followed he would be required at the very least to press the lady's hand adoringly, while if he followed his natural instincts he would catch the girl in his arms and kiss her breathless. Neither operation could be comfortably conducted in a phaeton. A little staff planning was obviously required.

Once he had remembered the ruined tower, this was simple. It was quite natural that he should wish to show his ward this relic of long dead Anderleys. Only the crumbling tower now remained of the original stronghold, destroyed during the Civil War and never rebuilt, since the reasons for choosing its hill-top site were no longer valid. But from that hill top a splendid view of all his wide domains could be had, and though he had no thought of dazzling his lady love with the magnificence of the offer he was making, he did have some notion of pointing out his great need of feminine support in the heavy task of wise administration. More important was the fact that the horses could be properly secured while the two of them admired the view, and his hands freed for more vital tasks.

Up to a point his well-laid plans worked admirably. Elizabeth was a little surprised when he turned up the narrow lane which led to the tower, but his explanation of its historic interest and of the extensive view to be obtained was well received. Indeed she was grateful for any impersonal topics and snatched eagerly at these, so that before he knew it he was plunged into a sea of historical narrative from which he had some difficulty in extricating himself. It was fortunate that the steep climb to the summit left her no breath to spare for further questions.

But having achieved the privacy essential to his plans, it was the Earl's turn to be tongue-tied. That was a difficulty which he had certainly not anticipated, but having dealt faithfully with the salient features of the landscape he found it impossible to turn the conversation to more personal topics. The reason was plain to see. Elizabeth was treating him as though he was some chance-met stranger, displaying the airy social manner that she had so unwillingly acquired at his own behest, and keeping him at arm's length with admirable dexterity. The warm intimacy of their shared vigil in Bassett's cottage, the dawning wonder and expectancy that he had recognised in her face as he had bidden her goodnight after that long ordeal might never have been, so sweetly distant was her manner. Having exhausted the conversational possibilities of the immediate vicinity, she was now enquiring, with every indication of eager interest, the names of the dimly seen Lakeland hills.

But even Elizabeth's social invention, when entirely unsupported, failed at last, and uneasy silence descended on the pair. To cover it she stooped and made an elaborate business of plucking a nosegay of the tiny yellow heartsease that starred the turf, and the Earl, in an attempt to bring the conversation back to a more human plane, chose to speak of Lucy.

"You will be glad to know that life has taken a happier turn for Lucy Bassett. It seemed to me desirable that she should be got away, for a time at least, from scenes that could hold only painful memories. I have found her a post with friends of mine in Knaresborough, and she is to go to them within the next few days. Bassett's sister is to go and keep house for him, so Lucy may have an easy mind as far as her father is concerned. In fresh surroundings one may hope that she will learn to forget. She is very young. Life could still hold some kind of happiness for her."

Before those fatal moments in the chapel when the scales had fallen from her love-blinded eyes, Elizabeth's heart would have glowed at this speech, so clearly expressing the almost fatherly concern that the Earl felt for his people. Now she saw in it only the cynicism of the cold-hearted man of the world. Lucy's day was done and she must be removed from the scene lest she prove an embarrassment.

Somewhere deep in her heart was a cold misery, a knowledge that she had lost something ineffably dear and precious, but for the moment disgust and rage were paramount and could not be wholly suppressed. Bitterly she said, "So now all is made tidy. A child has died and a girl's life is broken, but all can be set to rights by wealth and consequence. It is as bad as M. d'Aubiac's tales of the French court."

The Earl was taken aback, even a little hurt by this outburst. He knew that she felt deeply for Lucy, but that seemed no reason to rip up at him, who had honestly done the best that he could for the girl throughout her troubles. But at least she sounded more like his own warm-hearted impulsive Elizabeth rather than some shallow flibbertigibbet of a society damsel. He stooped beside her, where her fingers groped rather blindly for the slender stalks of the wild pansies, and caught her hands in his two strong warm ones.

"Elizabeth—dear Elizabeth—" Even in his eagerness he could not resist savouring the feel of her name on his lips. "What is it? What have I done? Only tell me what is distressing you so, and I swear I will put it right." He waited a moment, but she made no answer. "Even to the half of my kingdom," he went on softly, "all that remains to me. The rest is yours, my little love, if you will deign to accept it—if you will so honour me as to consent to be my wife," and he raised the unresisting fingers to his lips. "There is nothing I will not do to serve and pleasure you."

It was no good. She looked down at the fingers clasping hers—and remembered how Lucy had clasped and kissed them. The ghost of Lucy would always come between. His proud head was bent to hers, the grey eyes ablaze with love. "Say it, my darling," the deep urgent voice demanded. "Say, 'Yes, Richard, yes I will marry you.'"

If only she could fling herself into his arms in eager acceptance, forgetting everything but her own need and his nearness. Instead she must deny her heart and refuse the gift that was all her desire. And she must do it in such terms that he would never ask her again, for never again, she was sure, could she summon the fortitude to say no.

She withdrew her hands from his grasp and gripped them tightly together. Somehow she steeled herself to look him in the face as she said composedly, almost coldly, "While I deeply regret the need to give you pain, my lord, my answer must be no. You will perhaps recall that at our very first meeting I informed you that it was my intention to stay single."

Convinced as he had been that his love was returned, the shock was severe. But the Earl was not the man to give up at the first reverse.

"Such an intention may be changed," he said steadily, "and recently I have felt that you were not totally indifferent to me. If you will assure me that I am entirely mistaken in this notion, I will not trouble you further."

One simple little lie—and she could not bring herself to speak it. To do so would be to make him out a conceited coxcomb, and that at least he had not deserved. Surely she might spare him such humiliation? She said, "In less than two years' time I shall be free to do as I choose, and I have made up my mind that marriage is not for me. I mean to devote my life to the service of the poor and the unfortunate."

"There is no reason why you should not still do so as my wife," argued the Earl. "Indeed you would find such work much easier as a married lady. There are still many conventions restricting the conduct of single ones, especially when they are young and attractive. If you have taken me in aversion there is no more to be said, but I have learned to love you with all my heart and I believe that together we could make a life that would satisfy your desire to serve others and bring great happiness to both of us."

This was sheer torture. As so often before in their arguments she was left defenceless, for heart and mind alike agreed with his every word.

"I do not hold you in aversion, my lord," she said quietly, striving to achieve a temperate and dispassionate air. "Indeed I have learned to like you very well, and to value your judgement and advice. But such feelings are not a foundation for marriage. I have never known a father's sheltering care, and you have admirably filled that lack in my life. For this I am deeply grateful. But while I am fully sensible of the honour you have done me in seeking my hand in marriage, I cannot accept your very obliging offer."

The last part of this rather stilted speech was lost on the Earl. He had listened with grave attention and even a faint stirring of hope to its opening phrases. But the remark about fatherly care bit deep, for it had all along been his own secret fear that he was too old for the girl.

"You need say no more," he said quietly when she had made an end. "I regret the embarrassment I have caused you. Your position as my ward should have protected you from the distasteful task of having to refuse me. I can at least make some amends by promising that you shall not be troubled by further importunities."

That was what she had wanted, wasn't it? Wondering if hearts really did break under such a burden of wretchedness, Elizabeth said impetuously, "My lord, will you not let me go? It cannot be comfortable for either of us to be living under the same roof after what has just passed. Let me go home, at least for a little while," she ended pleadingly, as she saw his lips set in the old grim way that portended refusal.

He looked down at her gravely, the beseeching eyes, the quivering lips, and was swept by a wild impulse to lock her fast in his arms and kiss her into submission—let her see that he was not near so senile as she seemed to think. He could not do it, of course. He had already transgressed unforgivably, since she had a claim on his protection. But if this was to be his mood then he had best set her beyond his reach before he succumbed to temptation.

"Very well," he conceded, "it shall be as you wish. But not immediately. You are in no case to undergo the discomforts of so long a journey until you are fully recovered from the effects of your accident. Let us say in about ten days' time. That should give you long enough to recover your full health. Until then I fear that we must do our best to overcome any awkwardness that we may feel in each other's society. Fortunately Anderley is large enough. We need not meet except in company."

He took her arm with calm impersonality to steady her for the descent. Bitter desolation filled Elizabeth's heart as she submitted to this 'fatherly care' and to being installed once more in the phaeton. She longed only for her own room and the privilege of crying her eyes out in decent privacy. Instead she set herself to utter such commonplace remarks as her weary brain could devise in a gallant attempt to 'overcome awkwardness'.

Chapter Eighteen

The Earl was even better than his word. Several days passed, and Elizabeth did not so much as set eyes on him. Lady Hester casually let fall the information that he was staying with Mr Christison. The two of them were planning the installation of a steam engine at the mill so that there need be no more fear of unemployment in times of drought. Richard favoured the scheme and had offered to put up some of the necessary capital. His sister was a little surprised that he had deemed it advisable to take up quarters at Millthorpe, but of course he was getting older, and no doubt learning the wisdom of conserving his energies. Elizabeth winced.

Mr Elsford, too, was gone, having taken himself off to Manchester, of all unlikely places. Miss Bentley's Papa was known to have vast commercial interests in that rapidly growing town. So the household at Anderley had shrunk to a small feminine circle which offered little distraction to an aching heart.

They were at breakfast on the fifth day of the Earl's absence, and Lady Hester, following her usual practice, was regaling her companions with sundry choice items culled from the columns of the *Morning Post* as she sipped her coffee. Suddenly she stopped short, choked on a scalding hot mouthful, and rose to her feet, her rather protuberant eyes staring in blank disbelief at an announcement appearing in the columns of that highly respectable newspaper which she indicated with a trembling forefinger.

"I don't believe it," she gasped, having at last succeeded in swallowing the coffee. "It can't be true! Those odious Bentleys must have had the notice inserted. Timothy would never have allowed us to receive the first intimation of his betrothal through the columns of a newspaper!"

The paragraph which had so powerfully worked upon her Ladyship's emotions was the usual formal notice of the engagement between her nephew and Miss Bentley. Miss Trenchard shook her head gravely over the discourtesy of modern young people and ventured to hope that at least Lady Maria had received prior information of the interesting news.

"I'm sure that Richard knows nothing about it, or he would certainly have ridden over to tell me," declared the indignant lady. "And this is his heir! I vow it will serve the wretch right if Richard marries after all, for the thought of that silly little chit as the future mistress of Anderley is quite past bearing."

Elizabeth and Miss Trenchard said all they could to soothe and comfort her, but with little success. She must sit down at once to write a note to her brother, in case the announcement had escaped his notice, and a groom must carry it to Millthorpe, though quite what she expected the Earl to do about the affair was not made clear. But half-way through her epistolary labours she suddenly broke off, nibbling the end of her pen in silent brooding, the while she studied Elizabeth with a calculating gleam quite at variance with her usual amiability.

"And I shall tell him that it is his clear duty to marry," she suddenly announced, startling Elizabeth and Mary, who, thinking her absorbed in her letter, had been studying the offending notice and wondering how soon its appearance would bring down upon them a host of morning callers, all eager for further details which they would be quite unable to supply.

"He did once say something about reconsidering the position," mused Lady Hester, searching her memory. "Perhaps he foresaw this very situation. Yes! It was the night that the Bassett child died. I remember saying to him that a wife would have been of the greatest assistance in such an awkward situation, and he certainly said that he would think about it." She wrinkled her brow in the effort to recall further details of that conversation. Elizabeth could only stare and wonder. What sort of principles animated a lady who could calmly assert that a wife would be an asset in one's dealings with a discarded mistress?

The morning proved to be something of an ordeal. As they had feared, a number of highly interested neighbours had seen the notice in the papers, and there was a steady stream of callers offering felicitations and asking about wedding plans. Lady Hester rose to the occasion magnificently. There was no hint of disappointment or annoyance. Her smile seemed unaffected, her voice quite natural, as she spoke of the "naughty pair, taking us all by surprise, of course", and there was something graceful and amused about the impetuosity of youth and the news being quite delightful, and no, not in the least unexpected. One or two of the guests cast curious glances at Elizabeth and wondered if her pallor and subdued manner were the result of a disappointment over Mr Elsford, but since no one was so discourteous as to hint at such an idea, she remained in happy ignorance of their covert interest.

Nevertheless it was a relief when Harrison came to tell her that Lady Ann Ridsdale had called to enquire if Miss Kirkley would care to ride with her. Lady Hester smilingly consenting, Elizabeth thankfully excused herself and hurried out to greet this very welcome guest.

"Come and talk to me while I change," she invited. "Such an uproar as we have been in all the morning, I could not have been more thankful to be rescued. Half the county must have called to find out when the wedding was to be."

Ann gasped and stared, but before she could ask excitedly, "Whose wedding?" Elizabeth was enquiring if she had not seen the notice in the morning papers and went on to tell her about it, quite unaware that Ann had hoped for a far more interesting announcement.

It was good to be free of the house and cantering easily over the soft turf, and when eventually they pulled up to give the horses a breather, Ann had much to impart concerning the alterations at Millthorpe. She and Hugh had ridden over the previous day to watch the work in progress.

"I expect Richard will be taking you over to see the new engine when he comes home," she added innocently.

Elizabeth could think of nothing less likely, and said that she did not properly understand machinery.

"Mr Christison is to give a feast for all the mill hands the night before the engine is started," Ann went on. "It will be a great thing for them—no more short time in dry seasons—and he said they should celebrate in style, with buns and ale and dancing in the old tithe barn. I expect most of the Anderley servants will be going, too, since Richard is involved in the new venture." She chuckled. "You will have to wait on yourselves that night, unless you come to dinner with us."

Presently they turned the horses' heads homeward. Ann was a little in front or Elizabeth would not have chosen to ride along the lonely path that ran by Bassett's cottage. Someone was moving about in the garden enclosure. Lucy? She could not help shrinking from an encounter until she had grown more accustomed to her new knowledge. But the woman who was picking currants in the garden was middle-aged and a stranger to both girls, though she seemed to recognise them and bobbed a smiling greeting as the horses trotted by.

"What has become of Lucy Bassett?" asked Ann suddenly. "Are there new people living in the cottage?"

For the life of her Elizabeth could not prevent a certain amount of stiffness in her reply. "I think that must have been Bassett's sister," she said carefully. "I understand that Lord Anderley has arranged for Lucy to go to a post with friends of his in Knaresborough, in the belief that she would benefit from new surroundings."

"That is just like Richard," said Ann affectionately. "Nothing is too much trouble, no detail too small for him to see to it himself if it affects the welfare of his people. If there were more great landowners after his pattern we should hear less talk of revolution and a new social order."

Elizabeth made no comment, but Ann cheerfully accepted her silence as unquestioning support for her own opinion. After a reflective pause she went on in a more thoughtful voice, "And I daresay there is a little more to it than that. If Timothy Elsford brings his bride to Anderley I suppose it would scarcely do for Lucy to be living within a stone's throw, even if their child did die, poor baby."

There was a thundering in Elizabeth's ears that seemed to deafen and stun her. Through it she heard a beloved voice saying sternly, "She is as much a Scorton as you or I." Her eyes were blurred and her hands were slack on the reins, so that it was as well that she was riding the gentle Sylva instead of mischievous Jackstraw.

"Wh-what did you say?" she demanded incredulously.

Ann looked slightly conscious and coloured faintly. "I'm so sorry, Lizbeth. I thought you knew. Well—we all did—when you were so good about helping Lucy. Hugh said you were simply great, and that Richard had at last found someone worth—" She stopped, went scarlet, and plunged hastily for a safer topic. "We thought you must know that Mally was Timothy Elsford's child," she said bluntly. And then, seeing Elizabeth's white face, caught Sylva's rein and drew both horses to a halt. "What is it?" she begged anxiously. "What have I said to shock you so? Truly, Lizbeth, it wasn't so dreadfully wicked. He was only a boy, and spoilt and thoughtless, and Lucy, poor lamb, was a romantic dreamer. There was no question of rape, you know. They were just foolish boy and girl lovers. Richard was furious, of course—I don't think he has ever forgiven Lady Maria for not looking after Lucy better—but it couldn't be mended. He saw to it that Timothy settled a decent sum on her so that the child could grow up in modest comfort."

And die—and be buried in the chapel of her ancestors—because one man thought more of comforting a bereaved mother than of convention or public opinion. And she, ignorant, priggish Elizabeth Kirkley, had presumed to set herself up in judgement on him, and in so doing had wrecked her own hopes of happiness.

A hard little sob broke from her. She was not even aware of it. But Ann's friendly hand was grasping her arm and Ann's eyes were anxious as she repeated frantically, "What is it, Elizabeth? Are you ill? Should we go back to Bassett's cottage so that you can rest?"

A convulsive shudder shook her. Once before she had been taken to Bassett's cottage to rest, and that had been the beginning of it all. Now her tale was told. She had but to retire in her shamed misery to Gloucestershire, and never, never return to intrude upon the world of Anderley. In the deeps of self reproach she even prayed that she might escape without again setting eyes upon its owner. Feverishly she gabbled a weak excuse about a passing faintness and made an effort to pull herself together and behave normally, so that Ann was partly reassured. If she noticed that Elizabeth was very quiet for the remainder of the ride she had the good sense not to fuss over her with repeated enquiries. She was guiltily aware that her frank disclosures had proved more of a shock than she had expected, and this worried her, for since Elizabeth was not a mealy mouthed prude to be turning up her eyes in hypocritical horror at such a tale, it could only mean that in some way she was personally involved.

But how? Surely she could not have cared for Timothy Elsford? It was all very puzzling. She had been so sure that Richard had meant to propose on that carefully stage-manage drive *à deux*, and had daily expected to hear the news of a betrothal between the two. What could have gone wrong? Yesterday, Richard, behind his customary friendliness, had seemed strained and distant, and there was no mistaking Elizabeth's patent unhappiness, however she might try to hide it from her too perceptive friend. So both young ladies had good cause to wrap themselves in their own reflections, and parted presently in mutual goodwill and considerable misunderstanding.

Elizabeth was granted no opportunity for private brooding. They had been late in returning from their ride and already it was almost time to dress for dinner, which, in the absence of the master of the house, Lady Hester preferred to take early, country fashion. Indulgence in the orgy of repentance that might bring some relief would certainly leave tell-tale stains on her face. Somehow she must hold firm until it should be decent and reasonable to plead fatigue.

One fear at least could be dismissed as soon as she went into the dining-room. The small oval table in the window was set for three. So the Earl had not acceded to his sister's request that he should come home at once to discuss all the implications of Timothy's betrothal. He had, in fact, written to explain that he had been just on the point of setting out with Hector to inspect a working engine of a type similar to the one being installed at Millthorpe when her letter was brought to him, and since he could see no useful purpose to be served in fruitless discussion of what could not be mended, there was little point in breaking his engagement. He sent a civil message to his ward, trusting that she was now restored to her customary good health, and promising to put in hand the arrangements for her journey to Gloucestershire as soon as he came home. That would be in three or four days' time, on the morning after the Millthorpe feast.

It all sounded very kind and thoughtful—positively fatherly in fact—and Elizabeth wondered why a creamy feather-light syllabub should be so difficult to swallow.

Lady Hester, accepting her brother's defection in good part and becoming resigned to her nephew's matrimonial plans, chose now to turn her attention to Elizabeth's affairs. The latest news from Berkeley had shown Mrs Hamerton and Miss Clara to be going along famously, so why must Elizabeth go jauntering off to visit them just now? Soon there would be shooting parties and a great deal of informal entertainment going forward at Anderley. It would be a great pity for the girl to miss these promised treats. Luckily she did not seem to expect any answer to her plaintive monologue, and when dinner was done happily accepted Elizabeth's suggestion that she should write to her grandmother to confirm the promised visit while she and Miss Trenchard settled down contentedly to a game of cribbage.

Chapter Nineteen

Three more days dragged wearily by, long lonely days in which to dwell on a grey and desolate future, and to make matters even more depressing it rained without ceasing. Faithfully Elizabeth pursued her allotted course of study. It gave her the faint satisfaction of carrying out the Earl's wishes, even though he would never know of her meek devotion, and it had the added virtue of occupying her mind for at least some part of the day. She spent hours contemplating her situation, vainly seeking some way out of the tangle of her own creating. But there were two insuperable obstacles to any happy solution. The Earl had promised that she need not fear further importunities, and he would certainly keep his word. And even if she could ever summon up the courage to tell him frankly that she had mistaken her own heart, she could never, never confess the shameful truth. "Something that I overheard led me to believe that Lucy was your mistress, and of course I couldn't possibly marry a man like that." A fine way to set about convincing a man that you truly loved him!

She took to devising the most improbable sets of circumstances in which, by means unspecified, she and her guardian were alone together with everything explained and forgiven. Even shipwreck on a deserted island was not too ridiculous for her consideration, though whither they had been voyaging or how it came about that they two alone survived the disaster were unimportant details with which she did not trouble her powers of invention. These were, in any case, wholly absorbed in what happened next.

And she took to sleeping with one hand on a green jade ball beneath her pillow. On the night that Ann had told her the truth she had taken it from its place of banishment in the bottom drawer of the jewel cabinet, cradled its coolness between her palms and pressed it to a burning, tear-stained cheek. When she said farewell to Anderley she must leave it behind, but for these few remaining days she would take what comfort she could from the thought that his fingers had touched the lovely thing; that when he had sent it to her, it had been sent in love, and with the wish to make her his wife. But that last thought was only productive of more tears until finally she sobbed herself to sleep with the Chinese ball clutched against her breast.

It was sheer coincidence that the very next day she discovered the knack of the puzzle that had so defeated her at Greystocks despite Ann's patient explanations. The first time it happened she thought it was just a lucky accident and was much afraid that she would not be able to do it again. But her fingers seemed to go cleverly about the task almost of their own volition, and there was a completed ball in her hands again, its carved dragon regarding her surprised face with enigmatic oriental calm. Perhaps it was a good omen. Insensibly her depression lifted a little.

In this slightly happier mood she accompanied Miss Trenchard on the long-delayed drive to Little Cropton, and made a creditable attempt to enter into her companion's delight in its antiquities. But it was difficult to keep her mind from her own problems for long. The silver gilt Tudor chalice reminded her that the great Queen Elizabeth had died a spinster, while the tomb which enumerated the virtues and progeny of that long-dead mistress of Cropton Manor only served to press home the point that never, now, would she have children of her own. She had not thought that she had cared greatly for children, but Mally had taught her to know better. It was sad to say farewell to those fugitive fair-haired babies who had played one morning in the sunken garden at Anderley and held up grubby hands to catch the rainbow drops from the fountain. She set her lips firmly, and offered to help Mary make rubbings of the interesting brasses, even smiling a little over a memorial to a lad who died in 1753 and who 'knew arithmetick, geometry and astrology perfectly', and on their return home spent the rest of the day in sorting out her possessions and directing Edith as to which should be packed for her journey and which left behind as unsuitable for a simple country visit. It was a lowering occupation which did nothing to raise her spirits. She could not forbear casting wistful eyes on one or two specially loved gowns and wondering if she would ever see them, let alone wear them, again.

Friday brought a note from Ann, who had been afflicted with the toothache but was now much recovered except for a swollen face, which she did not want to flaunt abroad. She begged her friend to visit her and help beguile the tedium of her imprisonment. This Elizabeth gladly did. The rain had stopped at last so that she was able to ride over to Greystocks, and despite the nuisance of being obliged to take a groom, the exercise did her good. Ann, relieved of the acute pain of the toothache, was in hilarious mood, and they spent a cosy afternoon in planning the decorations for a ball to mark Hugh's coming of age in September. Elizabeth did not say that she was unlikely to be present on this auspicious occasion. Tomorrow would bring the Earl back to Anderley, and after that she guessed that her stay would be brief indeed. His prolonged visit to Millthorpe surely indicated that he found her continued presence in his home quite intolerable.

Lady Hester complained of a slight headache that evening and did not wish to indulge in her usual game of cribbage, suggesting instead that Elizabeth and Mary should give her the treat of a little music. Elizabeth, well aware that her own performance was no treat to anyone, least of all a lady with a headache, turned an imploring gaze on Mary and that kindly creature obligingly went to the pianoforte. She was no mean performer, having a soft clean touch and an insidious trick of sliding from melody to melody so that one never wearied. Lady Hester listened peacefully until her head nodded forward and she dozed off. Elizabeth drifted over to the window and stood with her brow pressed against the cool glass gazing out into a garden brilliant in the moonlight, absently tracking grotesque shadows to their sources until a familiar melody caught her attention. Mary was playing a waltz—the waltz that M. d'Aubiac had played the first time that she had danced with the Earl. Tears of foolish nostalgia gathered in her eyes, and since there was no one to see she made no attempt to force them back, so that for a moment or two she could not be certain whether she had really seen the queer creature on the terrace or whether its eccentric movements were a mirage produced by her tear-blinded gaze.

It was crippled in some way, for it was drawing itself forward on its forelegs and one hind leg was trailing helplessly. After two or three of these convulsive movements it would collapse and lie flat as though gathering strength for further efforts before renewing its painful progress. Strange that it should be making for the house and the brilliantly lit windows of the drawing-room instead of seeking the shelter of the dark shrubberies. And then the thing raised an agonised human face, a face that she recognised, and she was struggling frantically with the stiff window catch and running out on to the terrace.

His goal so nearly won and help in sight, Hanson had lapsed into brief unconsciousness, but some inner necessity, above and beyond the clamouring of his pain-wracked body brought him to his senses quickly enough. He wasted no time on expressing surprise at finding himself stretched out upon a sofa in his master's drawing-room, nor upon the anxious faces of the three ladies surrounding the foot of the sofa, nor even upon poor gasping Harrison, who had found John's inert weight a sore burden, even with the help of the two younger ladies. He directed a strained gaze at Lady Hester, and gasped out, "It's Mr Garrett, m'lady. Run amok. Fetch his lordship to me straight, for God help me, I cannot go to him."

Mary's eyes rounded in dismay, but Lady Hester remained calm. "His lordship is at Millthorpe. If you will explain just what is wrong I will have a message carried to him immediately."

If it were possible for a man already ashen grey to go even paler, John did so then, and a groan was wrenched from him that not all the pain of his own injuries had evoked. "Millthorpe!" he bit out. "That's where he's making for, unless I miss my guess, to blow up the mill dam."

Even Lady Hester was visibly shaken by this startling announcement, but checked her anxious questioning since John was painfully giving an account of having followed his charge on a wild cross-country chase after the manager of Coldstone quarry had come to him with a tale of a large quantity of gunpowder stolen from the explosive store. Garrett, forever hanging about the place, had naturally come under suspicion, and this was strengthened by his subsequent disappearance. But nobody could imagine what he wanted with the stuff until John remembered his earlier obsession with the mill dam and his vain attempt to open the sluices.

It seemed rather a forlorn hope, but it was the only possibility that anyone could think of, and John had saddled up and set out at once, feeling reasonably hopeful of overtaking his man, who, in spite of his long start, was on foot and heavily burdened. He had not done so. But Garrett, with the alerted instincts of the hunted, must have become aware of the pursuit and had promptly taken steps to counter it. He had holed up in a tree overhanging the track along which John was riding—"my eyes everywhere but where they should have been," John threw in ruefully—and had descended like a bolt from the blue upon man and beast, dragging John from the saddle, the horse bolting. Then they had fought—the issue never a moment in doubt, since not only was Garrett an exceptionally powerful man, but in his university days he had been a notable exponent of the manly art.

"Just played with me," growled John, with a reluctant, twisted grin. "Even said, polite like, that he didn't mean me no harm but he wouldn't have me interfering, and sent me to grass with as pretty a left hook as I'd like to see landed on somebody else's jaw," and his fingers reached up to explore the puffed, blueish bruise that was Garrett's mark. "What he didn't reckon for, if he meant no harm, was me breaking my leg through falling awkward-like across a stone. I made what shift I could to hobble along with a stick, but there was no bearing it"—apologetically—"so I just had to crawl. And that's the best part of an hour ago, and him well on his way to Millthorpe by now."

Lady Hester was prompt to take command. "Send one of the grooms here at once, Harrison," she said briskly, "and another for the doctor for Hanson's leg. There's no time to write a letter so send me an intelligent lad who can carry a message properly. And hurry, man," she ended impatiently. "What are you waiting for? This business is urgent."

"Milady," stammered poor Harrison, pop-eyed with consternation, "there's not a soul in the place to send except old Gentry, and he so crippled with the rheumatism he can scarce move faster than poor Mr Hanson here. They're all away to Millthorpe for the feast. And indeed, my lady, I'd go myself, but I've not crossed a horse since I was a nipper and I doubt I'd make a poor job of it." He was almost tearful about it, his face crumpled in lines of utter woe at the thought that for once he was quite incapable of carrying out his employer's commands with his usual smooth competence.

Lady Hester, who had completely forgotten the Millthorpe feast, bit her lip irresolutely.

"Never mind me, my lady," said Hanson. "I'll do well enough now I've no need to move. But someone must get word through to Millthorpe. If that dam goes it'll mean ruin to the standing corn, not to mention the stock that's grazing the water meadows, and maybe even one or two luckless souls swept away and drowned. It's not as though it was the usual kind of mill pool. They made it by damming the Essenthwaite beck where it runs through a little gorge. After heavy rain it builds up until there's a proper little lake there, and after the last three days I reckon it's pretty full right now." His eyes sought Elizabeth's in unspoken appeal.

As a child Elizabeth had once been taken by her grandfather to see the Severn bore, and the frightening sweep of that relentless wall of water had made a deep impression on her young mind, an impression strengthened by many a grim tale of the damage it could do. The thought of such a wave rolling down this peaceful valley was quite horrible.

"I'll go, John," she nodded at him with a cheerful grin. "Garrett—is that the name?—and an attempt to blow up the mill dam. Mary, will you come and help me change? Harrison, can you and Gentry manage to saddle a horse between you? I'll take Jackstraw—he's the fastest—but mind you pull the girths tight." She turned to smile at the worried Lady Hester. "Try not to be anxious for me," she said gently. "You can see that someone *must* carry the message, and there is no one else. I promise to be very careful."

But when she saw the animal that Gentry had saddled for her, even Elizabeth felt some qualms. "Seeing as it's a matter o' life and death," the bright-eyed ancient informed her, "I took and saddled Brigadier. That there Jackstraw," scornfully, "ain't 'ere no more. 'is Lordship giv' 'im away to the doctor the day after 'e threw you—along wi' a fair warning about 'is tricks, o' course. Wouldn't give the nasty brute stable room for so much as another day, 'e said. Now Brigadier, 'e'd never serve you such a trick. And if so be you've a fancy to go 'cross country to save time, why, 'e's a capital fencer, too."

The horse looked simply enormous in the moonlight. He was, in fact, just on seventeen hands, the Earl's favourite hunter, and Elizabeth had never ridden him because she had judged him far too big and strong for her. But there was no time to waste in changing. She must just make the best of it and pray that she didn't fall off, for she would certainly never be able to mount that equine cliff unaided.

But by the time that she had ridden down the avenue she knew that the old man had chosen well. The leashed power beneath her was completely responsive to her guidance. Brigadier's manners were perfect, his mouth like silk. With growing confidence she turned his head towards Millthorpe, thankful for the brilliant moonlight, for, whatever the risk, she must make speed, or she might as well never have set out. As her eyes grew more accustomed to the light she increased the pace to a full gallop. Brigadier might not be quite so fast as Jackstraw, but he had a pretty turn of speed for all that, and it did not seem long before they were passing the heather bank where Jackstraw had thrown her, and there was Anderley Old Tower, a ghostly finger pointing in the moonlight. Then she was coming up to the beautiful wrought-iron gates of Greystocks, and for a brief moment she wondered if it might not be wiser to summon help here. But two miles of tree-darkened avenue lay between gate and house, and the need for haste was predominant.

From now on it was new country. She knew the general direction of Millthorpe, and as Mary had sensibly pointed out, there would be plenty of light and noise to guide her to her actual destination. Brigadier raced on, making nothing of the light burden on his back, on and on through the night, his rider's every faculty alert to pick the safest way, until finally she left the road for the narrow lane that climbed steeply to the high moors where Millthorpe lay in the shelter of the encircling hills. Here she must steady Brigadier, for the going was rough, the lane deep-rutted by the heavy woolwains, and a stumble might lame her horse and bring the whole enterprise to ruin. She was nearing her goal now and within a few more minutes was clattering into the deserted village street. In the fields away to her right she could see a large building from which there issued, as Mary had foretold, noise and light aplenty. The only difficulty was that she could see no access gateway and she was in no mind to ride round looking for it. Deliberately she gathered Brigadier together and drove him at the tall hedge, felt the surge and lift of his leap and the thrust of his powerful quarters. Then they were safely over, and into a cornfield. Well—a breaking dam would do more damage by far than one horse in a cornfield. The farmer would just have to be compensated, that was all.

Several people were standing about the door of the great barn, cooling off after their exertions, and turned at the sound of the pounding hoofs, gazing open-mouthed at the sudden apparition of huge horse and dishevelled rider. Elizabeth's hat had fallen off as they leapt the hedge and her hair was tumbling about her shoulders. A voice from the shadows announced in startled accents, "Why! It's his lordship's Brigadier," and hands reached up to catch the reins as she drew to a halt and half slid, half fell from her lofty perch.

"His lordship?" she gasped breathlessly. "Yes, Miss, in here," said an unknown voice, and a sturdy arm was offered for her support as she stumbled a little, stiff from the long tense ride.

The Earl was standing with his back to her, but seeing the amazed faces all turning to gaze in her direction, swung round to seek the cause of the interruption. For one brief second she saw the grave countenance flash into eager delight. Then the glow faded and he was striding towards her.

"What is it, Miss Kirkley? What has happened?" he demanded imperatively. Hastily she poured out her tale. There was no need to fill in details. Before she was half done the Earl was racing for the door, calling instructions as he went. Everyone was to keep back. In inexperienced hands explosive was tricky stuff. He would tackle Garrett alone. But they must send messengers at once to the valley farms to warn of impending danger.

Men were scurrying in all directions. A huddle of startled women and talkative, excited youngsters gathered near the barn door, scarcely knowing what to expect. The Earl of Anderley took one look at his steaming horse, said, "Brigadier! Thank God!" and swiftly stripped off Elizabeth's saddle, vaulted on to the horse's back and galloped down the track that she had made in the corn. She saw the great chestnut rise smoothly to the hedge, and then horse and rider were gone. Presumably the dam and the danger lay in that direction. Once more Elizabeth acted in direct defiance of his lordship's orders. She forgot there was no gate. She simply gathered up her long skirts and ran as fast as she could after him.

The hedge would have defeated anyone less desperate, for it was thick and sturdy, but blessedly it was of beech instead of the more common hawthorn. She flung herself at it like a diver and clawed and wriggled her way across until finally she fell over on the other side into an overgrown and very muddy ditch, from which she emerged scratched and breathless, the skirt of her habit in ribbons, and, for a moment, not quite sure which way to turn. Then she remembered that she had seen no sign of a stream or a mill pool as she rode up the lane. It must lie downhill, beyond the village. She ran on again, flagging a little now and stumbling on the rough road, with a stitch in her side that made breathing difficult.

But here at last was the mill yard, the high iron-spiked gates standing open as the Earl must have left them, for not even Brigadier could have cleared such an obstacle. Now she must pick her way carefully, for the cobblestones were slippery with grease and there were bits of machinery lying about as traps for unwary feet. But the small gate across the yard was open and through it she could see the gleam of water, glass-still in the moonlight. That must be the mill pool, and at least the dam was still intact.

She had never seen a mill dam at close quarters and was amazed at the extent of the sheet of water that had built up behind this one. As John had said, it was almost a lake. She was surprised, too, to find quite a sizeable stream flowing from the foot of the retaining wall, not knowing that the sluices were open. But there was no time now to think of anything but the drama that was being enacted before her frightened eyes. A black silhouette in the moonlight, the Earl was standing on top of the wall close to the other side of the pool talking to a man who was kneeling among the stones that bordered the stream below him. The noise of the running water prevented her from hearing the words, but she assumed correctly that the kneeling figure must be the mysterious Garrett engaged upon his destructive business, and that the Earl was trying to persuade him to listen to reason. She had understood enough of Hanson's tale to know that the man was totally deranged, and guessed the Earl's task to be impossible achievement. Even as she watched Garrett turned his face up to the man above him, shouting something that she could not catch and hammering with his bare fist on the rock beside him. It did not need words to make plain the defiance in voice and bearing. She saw him fumble in the breast of his jacket and realised that he was trying to kindle a light. There was a spark and a tiny glow, and at the same moment the dark figure poised on the slimy wall crouched low and sprang, not for the kneeling man but for the creeping line of fire that led towards the charges he had laid, landed sprawling and rolled on it. Garrett leapt towards him, fists flailing, but the Earl managed somehow to twist himself away from the furious assault and regain his feet. There was a brief confused struggle on the moss-grown stones beside the beck, and then the Earl was down, and Garrett was scrambling up the opposite bank, disappearing among the trees as Elizabeth, not daring to trust herself to the slippery wall, started down the steep descent to the stream bed.

Chapter Twenty

She splashed through the water, regardless of the treachery of the deep pools, floundering and gasping as she missed her footing, but somehow struggling across to the other side, to the dark shape which was sprawled on the stones, so ominously still and quiet. Sobbing for breath, she fell on her knees beside him and tore open coat and shirt to lay shaking fingers over his heart. For a moment she could scarcely accept the message that frightened fingers conveyed to anxious brain. Then, in the wild exhilaration of relief, she flung herself face down across his body, covering the quiet face with passionate kisses and gathering the beloved head to her breast as she crooned foolish love words that fortunately there was no one to hear.

Then anxiety sprang up again. Even though he was alive, he might yet have sustained dreadful injury. A swift examination showed that, as far as her rudimentary knowledge went, there were no broken bones. But perhaps there were internal injuries, for surely it was not natural for a man to lie so long unconscious if he had only been stunned? There might even—a terrifying thought—be head injuries. Carefully, lightly, her fingers explored the shape of his head, and finding no obvious damage to account for his state laid open his shirt again to assure herself that his heart really was beating as strongly as she had first thought.

A calm deep voice spoke gently in her ear. "Quite unnecessary, my darling. Indeed I would willingly have reassured you sooner, since you seemed to be suffering a degree of anxiety quite disproportionate to my injuries. But one should never interrupt a lady, you know, and to speak truth I found your—er—remarks so absorbingly interesting that I should have been exceedingly loath to do so."

She had sprung back, startled and disconcerted, but at this point the inert figure came suddenly and fiercely to life. In one lithe movement he was on his feet and pulling her to hers, to catch her in his arms and return with interest the kisses she had bestowed upon him. For a moment, instinctively, she strained away, but on a soft little breath of laughter he only pulled her closer into his hold, and this time, in full realisation, she came willingly, holding up her mouth for his kiss with an innocent confidence that he found wholly enchanting.

After a little while he raised his head to look down at her. "The last time that we held private converse together," he said thoughtfully, "you refused my offer of marriage, and I promised not to pester you with repeated pleas. Well—I will not do so. It is no longer in question that you will marry me. You made that abundantly clear when you supposed me hurt or dying, and your kiss just now did nothing to counter the impression I had gained that for some unexplained reason you find me necessary to your happiness." And as she hid her face in his breast, overwhelmed with confusion that he should have heard her very explicit self-betrayal, he went on, with the note of laughter in his voice that she so loved to hear, "And don't try to fob me off with assurances that your affection is purely filial, for if it is, you outmatch even the oddities of Greek literature."

She glanced up enquiringly, puzzled at the reference, but he was looking over her shoulder at a group of people who were approaching the far bank of the stream and he went on cheerfully, "Furthermore, you no longer have any choice in the matter, for here comes about half my household, despite my strict orders, too, to discover us in this extremely compromising situation—and both of us in a state of undress that can only be described as most improper." He chuckled at her exclamation of dismay and would not permit her to release herself or make any attempt to tidy her person, assuring her that she would do very well as she was despite his teasing, and that the splash of mud on her left cheek was really so becoming that it was quite a pity that patches were no longer in fashion.

That made her laugh and look up at him with adoring, fascinated eyes. She had not guessed him capable of such light-hearted nonsense. The firm lips were curved in boyish mischief as he glanced over her head at the group of men who were now picking their way across the stream towards them. "Now, my girl," he said briskly, still holding her close to his side with an arm about her waist, "here's where we steal young Timothy's thunder."

Elizabeth looked at him blankly, never dreaming what he intended. The leaders of the rescue party halted uneasily a few paces away, uncertain as to whether they ought to intrude on so intimate a scene. The Earl raised his free hand in friendly welcome. "Here we are," he announced cheerfully, "both of us perfectly safe and no harm done. Some of you had best set to work to remove this gunpowder, and perhaps you, Burrows, would organise a search party for Garrett. He made off through the woods in the direction of Coldstone. Thanks to Miss Kirkley's warning, his scheme came to naught." He said nothing of his own part in the affair, listening gravely to his steward, who was suggesting that he should leave his horse for Miss Kirkley so that his lordship might ride Brigadier.

"Not a bit of it," said the Earl. "If you have to chase poor Garrett all the way to Coldstone, you'll need your horse. Brigadier shall carry double tonight if Mr Christison can find a saddle to fit him. Miss Kirkley and I will tidy ourselves a little at the Mill House and then make for home." He raised his voice slightly to make sure that his final sentence should carry to every member of his little audience. "I am in haste to tell my sister the good news that Miss Kirkley has done me the honour of consenting to marry me."

There was a moment of stunned silence. Then someone at the back of the little group—Elizabeth's young groom, Jacky—raised an irrepressible cheer in which the rest joined with gusto. There were wide grins on the moonlit faces and a babble of talk broke out. It seemed to be a matter of some doubt whether the urgent need to hurry back and tell one's wife or sweetheart the exciting news would not take precedence over more serious matters. After all—it would take a vast quantity of gunpowder to produce a more earth-shaking result! Discipline prevailed however, and only the steward came forward to offer his felicitations as the rest of the group dispersed to their various tasks.

"And now get out of that if you dare, my girl," said the Earl blandly, swinging his ragamuffin bride-to-be into his arms and making for the footbridge which crossed the stream some distance below the dam, and rejecting her protest that she was perfectly well able to walk with a cool assurance that he was perfectly well aware of it but preferred to carry her just the same. "No need to wait for the *Gazette* or the *Morning Post*. The news of *our* betrothal will be clear across the county before morning. Back out now, and you brand yourself a shameless jilt."

"Oh dear!" sighed Elizabeth, snuggling closer into his hold, "What *will* Lady Hester say? She was so cross about Timothy's behaviour."

"Never a word of dispraise," promised the Earl smugly, all conscious virtue. "For one thing she will be told the news before we send any announcement to the papers And in her letter to me on the subject of Timothy's betrothal she strongly urged the case for my early marriage. What is more, my love, she made it pretty clear just who she had in mind as my bride. She can scarcely raise any objection if I fulfil her wishes with a celerity that surprises her as much as it delights me."

They had reached the Mill House now, with kind Mr Christison fussing about them, offering every form of help and hospitality to the heroine who had done him such signal service, so there was no time for further private talk. His was a bachelor household, but he had already summoned his housekeeper, who surveyed Elizabeth's bedraggled appearance with horror and hurried her off to be dried and cleaned with sundry little clucks of sympathy and goodwill.

The habit was ruined beyond redemption, and since Mrs Mostyn was both shorter and stouter than Elizabeth, her kindly offers of a gown from her wardrobe were not very practicable. Eventually Elizabeth accepted the loan of a serviceable grey frieze cloak which covered the worst rents in the damp velvet and gave her a sober Quakerish air. With the mud washed from her face and hands and her hair neatly braided into a coronet she came down to join the Earl and Mr Christison, to be put to shame at once by her lover's extremely *point-de-vice* appearance. He had the advantage of her, of course, in that he had plenty of spare clothes available at the Mill House, and had changed his scorched and moss-stained pantaloons and soaked jacket for immaculate leathers and riding coat.

"I know, my love, I know," he said defensively, coming to meet her and taking her hand to lead her to the fire. "But one of us at least ought to make an effort to keep up appearances." And as Mrs Mostyn withdrew curtsying, to bring the sherry and the Madeira that Mr Christison had called for upon her entry, he added wickedly in her ear, "And that rig-out of yours will be just the thing for prison visiting."

There was no chance to retort as he deserved. Her host was enveloping her slender fingers in his huge paw and expressing his delight in the news which his young friend had just confided to him. He only regretted that it must snatch them away so soon, for of course Lady Hester must be told at once, but he pledged their future cheerfully in a bumper of Madeira and hoped that he might soon be permitted to welcome them to his house with all the proper formalities.

It all seemed dreamlike to Elizabeth, sipping her sherry while her still damp habit steamed before the rosy log fire. Warmth and the wine on top of her recent exertions were lulling her to drowsiness. But presently their goodbyes were said and the Earl was swinging easily into the well-worn saddle that someone had unearthed for Brigadier. Obediently she set her foot on his as instructed, and helpful hands tossed her up to him. Mr Christison called farewells, concealing his amusement at a state of mind which had caused his sober, hard-bitten friend to refuse all offers of a comfortable carriage in favour of carrying off his willing captive across his saddle bow, and they were trotting gently down the drive towards the lane.

It was tempting to yield to the bliss that enfolded her and lie content in the curve of his arm. But something still had to be done. She could not be truly happy until she had confessed her grievous fault; and it would be easier now, alone in the quiet dark. She struggled to raise herself a little and was instantly supported.

"What is it, my darling?" he said softly.

She sought for words. "My lord, there is something I must tell you. Something I have to confess," she brought out at last.

"The name is Richard, beloved, as well you know. And whatever your confession—from murder to high treason—I will not have you call me 'my lord'."

"Richard," she said, softly, lovingly, as she had murmured it against his closed eyelids in the shadow of Millthorpe dam.

He drew her closer, settling the top of her head beneath his chin, and said quietly, "And this terrible confession? What is it, then?"

That was not so easy. She thought about it carefully. Then—"Not murder—but high treason—yes."

His voice was warm and kind and faintly amused as he said, "High treason against whom, sweetheart?"

"Against you, my l— Richard," she said humbly.

"How very shocking! Would you like to set out the charge in detail?" invited the velvety voice in the darkness.

He had to wait a long time for the answer, but presently, timidly, for somewhere in the region of his heart, a meek voice said, "I thought you were Mally's father."

Perhaps on any other occasion the Earl would have been as shocked and hurt as she had feared. But her confession came when he was at the very zenith of happiness. The past week had been utterly wretched. Each morning had brought only the prospect of a lonely future, filled with the familiar duties and responsibilities that made up his life, and bereft of the hopes that had lately tantalised him with the promise of warm happiness. Then Elizabeth had come, riding out of the night, and there had been danger and the need for swift action, and now she was here in his arms, his to hold and cherish. Nor was he in any doubt that he had won her heart. It was not the Earl of Anderley that she had consented to marry, else she had never refused him the first time, but the man himself whom she had found indispensable to her happiness. And this realisation transformed his world. He seemed to recapture the lightheartedness of youth. The most serious matters developed an unexpected comic twist, and he had suddenly made the surprising discovery that there was something good and lovable about every single member of the human race.

He was, he hoped, a reasonably modest man, but he could not help being aware that most of his elders held him up as a positive pattern card of moral rectitude, which somewhat reasonably caused the younger and more frivolous members of local society to judge him as virtuous to the point of starchiness. It took his innocent, adorable Elizabeth to cast him for the rôle of a *roué* so heartless that he had introduced his intended wife to his cast-off mistress and permitted her to nurse their base-born child.

It was too fantastic to be anything but funny. He tried hard to control his unseemly mirth, knowing that the poor little scrap in his arms—she was five foot seven in her stockinged feet—was awaiting his judgement in genuine anxiety, but it was too much for him. His head went back and he emitted such a hoot of laughter that even Brigadier's ears twitched backward as though he wished to share the joke.

"Oh no, my darling! No!" he gasped at last, still shaking with laughter. "If *you* regarded me as your father—or pretended to"—with an admonitory little shake for past folly—"poor Lucy thinks me her grandfather at least, with a touch of patron saint thrown in, though certainly more patron than saint." By a truly heroic effort he managed to suppress the rising tide of laughter, and went on more soberly, "I gather that you now know the truth, so I will say only that I have tried as best I could to help the poor child out of her difficulties. But what in the world gave you such a very peculiar notion?"

A shamefaced Elizabeth explained how it had all come about. "And you will forgive me?" The voice was so very low that he had to bend his head to catch the words, and seized the opportunity to kiss the tip of her ear, trusting cheerfully to Brigadier's good sense.

"No forgiveness needed," he said teasingly. "I can only be grateful to the mischievous Gods. Just consider! However strong the evidence, never again will you dare to think ill of me! Under such auspicious circumstances our married life should indeed be blissfully happy!"

The reins fell slack on Brigadier's neck as gentle fingers tilted Elizabeth's chin so that she might be adequately forgiven, but that wise animal trotted on cheerfully. He was heading for home. What matter the folly of the human creatures on his back?

Chapter Twenty-One

They were all gathered under the great cedar. As the Earl had foreseen, the news had spread like wildfire, but, since there was as yet no formal announcement, they were spared the formal visits of congratulation. That had not, of course, prevented Ann and Hugh from riding over immediately after breakfast, the news having reached them the previous night. Ann, vowing that she had predicted the eventual outcome weeks back, announced that she had come to assert her claims to being bridesmaid, while Hugh was quite overset when the Earl asked if he would be his groomsman; seeing which, the Earl took pity on him and explained that he had only thought of requisitioning his services because he was so conveniently to hand, and so they would be able to brush through the whole business more expeditiously, a courteous explanation which set Hugh quite at his ease. He grinned, and aimed a playful punch at his friend's ribs, the Earl covering up promptly and begging him to desist, since that was just the spot where Garrett had landed the punch that had winded him the night before.

"You seem to have played a very gallant part in last night's little episode," jeered Hugh, getting his own back. Elizabeth's eyes sparked at that, but before she could utter indignant protest the Earl caught her eye and said, "No you don't, my girl. If you dare say one word, I shall tell them just how I was prevented from leading the pursuit," and Elizabeth subsided meekly, to the deep disappointment of their interested friends.

The two girls drifted into a discussion of clothes, Ann saying mischievously that she had a particular fancy for a tint that was neither apricot nor gold but somewhere between the two, and did Elizabeth think it would be becoming to a brunette bridesmaid? "Just the colour of that rose in your sash," she explained with an air of complete innocence.

The doctor's gig appeared round the curve in the avenue and he waved cheerfully in passing and presently came back to say that Hanson's leg was doing just as it ought. "A clean break, and doesn't seem to have taken much harm from the mauling it got, which is a merciful dispensation of Providence, my lord."

"Yes, indeed," agreed the Earl. "John is the real hero of the occasion. Pluck to the backbone. Always was."

"But a sad business about Mr Garrett," the doctor went on. "Or perhaps I should not say so. It may have been all for the best, for indeed, my lord, you would have had to agree to his being confined after this latest exploit, and that, you have always maintained, would be worse than death."

The Earl nodded but did not pursue the subject, and the doctor, after one or two enthusiastic comments on his gift horse's paces and behaviour, took his leave.

Elizabeth looked up at the Earl, a hint of penitence clouding her happy face. "What happened to Mr Garrett?" she enquired. "I'm afraid I'd forgotten all about him."

"I did not think there was any need to distress you with the story," he said. "The doctor is probably in the right of it when he says that it is better this way, so do not grieve for him too much. The men found him at the quarry foot early this morning. Perhaps he slipped or missed his way in the darkness. He must have been killed instantly and could not have suffered." Privately he considered it more than likely that Garrett had deliberately flung himself to his death, but there was no point in dwelling on that sort of speculation. Deliberately he broke the sympathetic little silence, asking Hugh if he felt inclined to embark at once on his new responsibilities by accompanying him into Gloucestershire. "For this insubordinate wench of mine declares that she'll not be married without her grandmother and her aunt to see the knot fairly tied. And for my part I'd as lief they saw for themselves that she is marrying me of her own free will and not as the result of blackmail or any other kind of tyranny," he added with a reminiscent little smile in Elizabeth's direction.

"Why yes!" said Hugh innocently. "I had forgot you are her guardian. I say, Anderley, it's not at all the thing to marry your ward. Did you ask your own permission?"

"It was a very delicate situation, my dear Hugh," expounded the Earl solemnly. "She wouldn't have Timothy. I did once think that she might even take a fancy to you, but clearly she has a little more discrimination than the average female. So what could I do but marry her myself? Couldn't have her hanging on my hands, you know. People would say I hadn't done my duty. And since she has become quite docile and biddable under my training, I managed to bring myself to sticking point—"

The end of this eminently reasonable exposition was lost, two highly incensed young ladies pelting the speaker with cedar cones with such unfeminine accuracy that he fled as fast as his long legs would carry him with Elizabeth in hot pursuit. With deep cunning he led the chase around the corner of the house, stopped short, and turned about to catch the flying figure in his arms and fold her close, breathless with running so that she must needs submit to his kisses. Then he held her off for just a moment, his hands framing her face, as he said with new-learned diffidence, "You do come to me willingly, don't you, my darling? It wasn't quite all funning back there. I'm too old for you, I know, and selfish to claim you for my own when you've seen so little of the world. But indeed I cannot bear to give you up."

Confidently the blue eyes smiled back into his. She gave her head a comical little shake. "Not willingly, my lord. More than that. In despite of myself, for try as I would, I could not help but love you. So I come to you proudly, eagerly, and with all my heart."

If you enjoyed *A Match for Elizabeth*, please share your thoughts on Amazon by leaving a review.

For more free and discounted eBooks every week, sign up to our newsletter.

Follow us on Twitter, Facebook and Instagram.

23215310R00087

Printed in Great Britain
by Amazon